Amish Sisters Marry

Becca's

Boy

Book 1

By Rose Doss

The sale of this book without its cover is unauthorized. If you purchased this book without a cover, you should be aware that it was reported to the publisher as "unsold and destroyed". Neither the author nor the publisher has received payment for the sale of this "stripped book."

Copyright © 2022 by Rose Doss. All rights reserved.

Without limiting the rights under copyright reserved above, no part of this publication may be reproduced, stored in or introduced into a retrieval system, or transmitted, in any form, or by any means (electronic, mechanical, photocopying, recording, or otherwise) without the prior written permission of both the copyright owner and the above publisher of this book.

ISBN: 978-1-955945-42-4

Cover images courtesy of period images and canstockphoto
Interior image from Brandi Lea designs
Cover by Joleene Naylor.

Manufactured/Produced in the United States

CHAPTER ONE

Becca shaded her eyes, squinting up at the large skeleton of a barn just raised that late spring morning. The structure sprawled now, attached to a large side section with a lower single-story roof. As the Yoder farm was bigger than most, more barn area was needed for hay and horses.

At first light, the field behind the *Haus* had been empty. As lunch approached, the frame of the enormous farm building had already been lifted to the sky. Along with dozens of other straw-hatted *Menner*, her older *Bruder*, Adam, sat now dangling on a rafter.

At least, she thought it was him. Becca waved again at the *Mann*, hoping Adam got the message to come down and eat the mid-day meal.

From her spot in the grassy field behind the *Haus*, she stared up at the tall, gaunt structure. To her pleasant surprise, a *Mann* on the rafters took off his hat and waved it at her.

Adam. Apparently, he'd seen and accurately read her message. That was the great thing about him. She was closest to this *Bruder* because they seemed to share the same thoughts, at times.

Behind her, women brought out platters of meats and vegetables, along with plates of bread and butter for the industrious crew, loading the long tables. The women's chatter as they worked filled the shaded area behind the *Haus* and Becca smiled at the contented sound. The busy kitchen area inside had been warm and crowded with friends and family gathered to chop vegetables and fry up the meats to power the *Menner* in their labors.

1

Becca waved again, receiving another response from the speck at the top of the structure.

"You know that's not Adam, right?"

Whipping around, she saw Saul Stutzman right behind her. Adam's best friend—after her—the solid, tall, brown-haired *Mann* grinned at her and she smirked back at him.

She had no issue with Adam's other friends, but Saul irritated her and seemed to go out of his way to achieve this.

As did the other *Menner* working there, Saul wore no coat, suspenders over his white shirt that was sweat-stained after a morning of heavy labor. He'd apparently just gotten a drink from the water barrel at the back corner of the Yoder *Haus* as dampness clung to his dark dowsed head, droplets clinging to his tanned cheeks and splashing down the front of him. A broad straw hat dangled from one lean hand.

"It is Adam," she snapped. "I see him plain as day."

"Nope. Adam's working over on the side section. I've been working beside him all morning and just came down for water. We've helped raise the rafters on the side section. Whoever you're waving at isn't Adam, although he looks very friendly. Maybe you have an admirer."

The irritating *Mann* beside her gave Becca a teasing smile. "You should wait here and see who it is."

"Do you think I don't know my own *Bruder*?" she shot back, glaring at him.

Saul laughed, throwing his head back in amusement. "I'd think so, but apparently you don't."

"Why don't you get back to work?" Becca scowled up at him, wishing not for the first time that she could add inches to her small frame. Even though *Gott* had directed them to be kind to all, she found Saul to be very annoying. She wished she didn't, but there it was.

"And miss the great lunch you women have made for us?" Saul said.

2

Becca had already started walking back toward the *Haus*. Thankfully, her friends Anna and Rachel were in the kitchen. Unfortunately, Saul fell into step beside her.

"We always have such *gut* dinners," Saul commented, rubbing his flat stomach with a large hand.

Sending a sideways glance towards the tall, solid *Mann* walking beside her, Becca noted, "You don't seem to have missed many meals."

Saul chuckled, not seeming fazed by her snide words. "I don't generally miss meals. That bread I saw Chloe Nissly putting out looked *gut*."

"I'm sure everything is good." Although she doubted Chloe's was as good as her own. Only Anna could come close to Becca's natural baking skill. Of course, it wasn't for her to say, but she knew it to be true.

Saul's teasing remark had to address the area of baking at which Becca knew she did well. Baking was her hobby and her greatest strong point. Pretty much, her only strong point, she reflected, a shade sadly. She did that well, though, and it was totally typical that Saul chose to tease her about another *Maedel's* bread.

Becca had never understood why sunny, friendly Adam and sarcastic, quieter Saul were such good friends. At first glance, they had little in common. Of course, *Gott* wanted them all to be kind to others, but this went far beyond His command. The two *Menner* had been friends since childhood and it was all well and good to say that their community was separate unto themselves, but Sugarcreek had a large Amish population. Surely, her *Bruder* could have found a friend who fit with him better.

Not that it was any of her business, she reminded herself hastily. *Gott* also told them to look for the plank in their own eyes, not the mote in others'. Still, since she'd finished school four years ago and spent more time at home when she wasn't at work, she'd seen how often Saul dropped by the Zook *Haus*.

The two of them walked toward the house together, silence falling between them. Saul wasn't a big talker and didn't seem uncomfortable with this, but it was awkward and unnatural to the naturally out-going Becca. After wracking her brain, she finally asked, "Do you know if Adam is coming in to eat?"

Slanting her a glance, Saul said, "I'm sure he'll come down for water and to rest."

"*Gut.*" The two approached the back of the Yoder *Haus*, Saul sauntering off to chat with a group of other *Menner* under a tree.

Before he was out of earshot, he said, "Nice chatting with you."

Becca looked after him, her mouth thinning. She'd never understand him and found him annoying, even though they were told not to be critical of others. Usually, this wasn't a problem of hers.

Across the yard, she saw Chloe Nissly waving at her—over the plate of bread Saul had noted—and she stretched her own lips into a smile as false as she knew Chloe's to be. Becca knew her baking skills were better than average. She'd been told this often enough. Her own bowl of fresh baked rolls were on the tables, too, but she had absolutely no need to point that out to Saul.

Chloe could preen herself to her satisfaction. There was no way her bread was better than Becca's. Even though Becca had lots of friends, Chloe had been her competitor since the girls were small. Becca didn't wish Chloe harm, but it still rankled that Chloe seemed to want to best her in every way. It was annoying, too, that the girl seemed so confident of her skills.

Becca thought she just needed to spend more time with her sisters—Abigail, Eve, Naomi and little Faith—and her good friends Anna and Rachel. They all liked her. Sometimes she thought they liked her more than she liked herself!

"It's always so nice to see our friends and family," Beth Zook said comfortably to her husband as the Zook's buggy jogged home after church at the Fisher *Haus* the next Sunday.

Becca sat in the buggy seat behind her *Mamm* and *Daed*, beside her eldest *Schweschder*, Abigail. Their *Bruders*, Noah and Ezra, occupied the buggy's third seat and Adam, the oldest Zook son, drove another buggy behind them with *Grossmammi* Ruth and the rest of the *familye*.

The sun had begun to sink in the August sky and, as it faded, the fields they trotted past were gleaming green and leafy in the dusk.

"Must you bounce around in the seat so?" Abby's question to her held a low note of reproof, speaking so their *Eldre* in the front seat and their *Bruders* in the seat behind didn't hear.

Becca leaned over to give her oldest sister a squeezing hug. "I had such fun today with our friends, didn't you?"

"Of course," Abigail wiggled her shoulders for release. "I'm just ready for some quiet…and you bouncing around in your seat isn't quiet."

"Sorry," Becca chirped. "I just love seeing everyone."

"I know."

Her sister always sounded just tolerant of her and Becca had gotten used to this, knowing that she could sometime be a handful.

"*Mamm*?" Becca scooted forward on her seat to speak with her mother. "Is *Grossmammie* Ruth making her special beets for supper tonight?"

"She is," Beth Zook turned to confirm.

"Just look at that field of corn," *Daed* interjected. "*Gott* has given us land that is fertile."

"If only it was cheaper to acquire," Abby said, looking in the direction their father had gestured.

"This is true." Able Zook gave a gusty sigh. "Many cannot afford to buy land unless it's passed on within the family."

Looking over his shoulder, he commented, "Saul Stutzman, Adam's friend, has the right idea. He was telling me and Adam that he's using the profits from the family farm to buy up smaller parcels of land to help his younger *Bruders* establish their own places. It's the only way they'll get farms of their own."

"That's kind of him," Abigail remarked in her calm voice.

In the seat behind where she and Becca sat, their brothers seemed to be wrestling in rowdy boy style.

"I understand that Saul has dedicated several of his fields to growing organic crops," Abigail commented.

Hanging over the back of the driver's seat, Becca looped her arms around her *Mamm*.

"*Yah*," Able chuckled, his wide shoulders shaking. "It's the *Englischers'* new thing—organic food."

"Food is food," his *Frau* stated with a touch of Abigail's calmness. "*Gott* gave it to us to make us strong. This organic nonsense is just that."

"I don't know, Beth," *Daed* said. "I think Saul is *schmaert* to try this. It's always *gut* to explore new ways to bring in more money. Adam told me this is helping Saul afford land purchases for his *Bruders*."

Becca gave her *Mamm* a squeeze before sliding back in her buggy seat. "He may be *schmaert* in this way, but Saul can also be annoying. Really annoying."

"I don't know if I should tell you." Chloe simpered, pausing as she lifted the butter churn handle several days later.

Becca had known the *Maedel* since their school days and, although Chloe's tendency to exaggerate was well-established, Becca impetuously put out a hand. "You know I can keep secrets! Of course, you can tell me."

She didn't particularly like Chloe, but the implication that she couldn't keep her mouth shut was untrue and unfair.

An errand to take some special-made cheese from the Zook *Haus* to Chloe's *Mamm* had led Becca to stop by the Nissly place on her way to work at an *Englischer*-run B & B, The Sunflower Inn. While Becca waited for the gift of rolls that Chloe's *Mamm* wanted her to take back to her mother, she had fallen into conversation with Chloe. As her schoolmate was working in the

Nissly kitchen while her older and younger sisters did chores outside the *Haus*, they were alone.

"We aren't to brag about such things," Chloe said with a shy smile, as if she wanted her secret dragged out of her.

"Fine," Becca retorted, tired of the game and not interested in adding to Chloe's already high self-opinion, "don't tell me then. Are you coming to the Sing that the Guth family is having after our next church service?"

"Well," Chloe assumed a bashful expression as she lifted the churn's paddle, "Thad hasn't said, but I expect I will and that he'll want to drive me home."

"Thad?" Becca responded, trying to keep curiosity out of her voice.

She and Chloe had gone to school together with Thad Oberholtzer.

Although they both lived in Sugarcreek and saw him at church, Becca hadn't given Thad much thought. He'd always been nice enough, not nasty and taunting as were some *Buwes*. She felt sad at the thought that such a nice boy was apparently now chasing Chloe. The *Maedel* did like making a show of things, even if they were directed to do otherwise.

"Are you and Thad courting?" As soon as the question was out of her mouth, Becca knew she shouldn't have asked. Courting was a private matter. It wasn't spoken about. Still, Thad and *Chloe*? He could do a lot better than waspish Chloe.

Bracketing the churn between her knees, her muted sage green skirt bunching up around her, Chloe kept the churn handle moving.

She giggled. "He's a very attractive *Mann* now, not that the outside of a person matters, of course."

"Of course," Becca responded in a mechanical voice.

"You know—besides being very Godly and having just recently joined the church after he returned from his *rumspringa*— he will be given his father's feedstore. Along with his brothers, of course.

The impressive manner with which Chloe made this announcement left Becca with the urge to roll her eyes. She resisted it barely, saying, "Thad's always been nice."

A superior smile crossed Chloe's face and she asked with concern, "Are you courting with a *Buwe*?"

The whole conversation was against everything they'd been taught about plain living, but Becca couldn't help feeling ruffled by the question. More than anything, she wanted to assure Chloe that she was seeing someone...a *Mann* as nice and with as prospects as *gut* as Thad.

She knew she shouldn't let the other girl get to her, but the urge was strong.

"It's just as I hoped," Chloe said smugly. I believe Thad and I have liked one another since we were children."

Chloe's self-satisfaction revolted Becca.

"Funny. I don't recall you playing together much," she commented in a musing voice, stifling her urge to make a face at the girl.

"Oh, yes. We were just very private."

"As *Kinder*?"

"*Yah*. I think we've always known though."

Becca had had quite enough of this nonsense. "Known what?"

"Why, that we would end up together."

"Thad and you have agreed to marry?" She should probably have been less blunt, but Chloe's exaggerated claim irritated her. Becca shrewdly knew things hadn't progressed this far.

"I don't think we should talk about this." Chloe glanced down with what Becca saw as assumed modesty.

"Then, you probably shouldn't have brought it up," she said with less annoyance than she felt. Chloe was always trying to best her, seeming to delight in this.

Becca was tired of it.

"What are you doing in here?" Saul asked in a caustic voice several days later with the total lack of deference due a girl who'd tagged at his and Adam's footsteps all through childhood.

He actually liked giving his friend's sister a hard time. Becca was such a spicy, lively *Maedel*.

Giving him a sarcastic smile, she ignored his question now, continuing into the Zook barn to sit on one of the straw bales stacked there.

As if Saul hadn't said anything, Adam kept forking straw into the different stalls, returning to their previous conversation. "And you think this organic farming is likely to make *gut* money?"

"It is from my experience," Saul said. "I started with smaller crops several years ago and have begun doing this on a larger scale. It's not hard, once you understand the process."

"What are you talking about?" Becca wiggled to settle herself more completely on the straw bale.

"You have no business here," Saul retorted. "Why don't you go into the *Haus* and ask you *Mamm* what she needs you to do?"

"I have just as much right in our barn as you do. More right." She smirked at him.

"Leave her alone, Saul," Adam intervened absently before adding. "And farming this way is truly making you extra money?"

"Enough extra here and there to buy several small parcels of land. I'm gradually putting together a farm for Abe now that he's almost grown."

"That's *schmaert*," Adam kept moving the pitchfork to loft hay into the feeding racks. "It's very *gut* that you can do this to help your *Bruders* continue farming. I've heard that Stephen Yoder has begun training at a feedstore job in town. His *familye* can't afford a farm for him."

Becca wiggled to settle more comfortably on the hay bale. As long as she could remember, Adam and Saul had been good friends. She couldn't say why this was so, but their friendship had thrust Saul into the Zook *familye*. He was such an easy target for her remarks that she'd gotten used to their sparring back and forth.

He was hard to read, though. His sturdy face looked out from the wide straw hat he wore, giving nothing away.

His stoicism irked her out-going soul and made her want to laugh at him. Thank heavens he had no notion of the state of matters between her and Chloe Nissly. She could only imagine how much Saul would look for ways to compliment Chloe, and thereby, put Becca down. The very thought had her irritated.

CHAPTER TWO

"*Argh*!!" Making a sound of frustration, Becca shaded her eyes from the afternoon sun several days later as she plucked futilely at the blackberry brambles that gripped her long, gray skirt. A basket full of juicy blackberries dangled from the crook of her arm.

Tugging to get free, she found the thorny bushes had snagged the other side of her skirt, as well.

Becca tilted her head to the sky, suddenly feeling tears press behind her eyes. Her plan had been so simple—pick some blackberries and bake a pie for the Oberholtzer *familye*--Thad's family. She was a *gut* baker, she knew, and didn't *Gott* tell them to be kind to others?

Jerking at her skirt again, she kept the basket of berries right side up, registering that she was completely snared! How had this happened? She'd picked berries from this very bush a hundred times!

She didn't want to reflect too much on Chloe's claim that Thad was spoken for. It most likely wasn't true, anyway. Typical Chloe. From what Becca had seen, there was no evidence of them courting and—and a pie never hurt anyone!

Besides, Thad had always been nice to her. He deserved a pie.

If only she could get out of this bush!

Gott! Please help!

Jerking at her skirt, Becca made another irritated sound when the fabric held firm.

"What the heck are you doing?"

She closed her eyes in frustration, releasing a breath. Becca knew that voice. Of all the annoying *Menner*…

Saul laughed a deep, rusty sound, coming round into her sight. "My goodness, woman. You have gotten yourself into a *bickle*. Why did you walk right into the bush?"

"I didn't walk into the bush and you have no business saying I got myself into this pickle!"

"Okay." He circled the bush, grinning, his straw hat pushed back a little on his head.

He must have been working in the fields because he again wore only a shirt and pants, his jacket apparently having been discarded in the day's warmth.

"Your farm isn't near here. In fact, it's to the other side of our *Haus*," she snapped. "What are you doing here?"

"Rescuing you, apparently," he responded, standing at the edge of the bush and pulling the ensnaring brambles aside carefully.

She glowered at him, the full basket of berries on her arm. Summoning as much dignity as she could muster in her imprisoned state, the blackberry thorns holding her tight, Becca drew in what she hoped was a calming breath, lifting her chin.

This was an incredibly embarrassing position for Saul, of all *Menner*, to find her.

"*Yah*," he responded, still grinning as he steadily worked to get her loose. "Lucky for you that we've bought some land nearby that will be a good start on a farm for Ben."

From her immobilized position, she could only say with what she hoped appeared to be casual disinterest, "Abe is older. Shouldn't he get a farm first?"

"*Yah*." Saul had worked his way toward her and pushing aside each bramble, he now carefully freed her skirt from the thorns ripping into her it. "Abe's land is north of here."

Becca stared at him. Farms were pricey and many had left the land entirely, not being able to buy their own. "How did Abe manage to get land? Did your *Daed* set money aside for his farm?"

"Some." Saul didn't look up from his task. "We were able to add to it, as well."

This, at least, was a neutral topic.

"You mean you were able to add to it," she said, reluctant to admit it, but knowing she needed to give even her tormenter his due. "Everyone knows you've run your family farm since your *Daed* died."

His head still bent over the bramble bush holding her tight, he shrugged. "It's been a *familye* farm. We've all worked it. Not just me."

"Maybe," she commented, "but you're the oldest. You've been at this the longest and the oldest usually gets the family farm, if they want it."

"Hmmph," he grunted, not lifting his head from his task.

"Even my *Mamm* has talked of how you've helped your mother and your *familye*."

Saul looked up from his spot in the bush next to her as if she hadn't spoken, the thorny branches held aside by the broad stance of his sturdy thighs, "These berries had better be worth all this."

Hearing his implied criticism, she retorted, "They're the best and sweetest blackberries around here. I need them for a special pie I'm baking."

"A pie? Who for? The *Englischer* bed and breakfast where you work?"

He was so close that he blocked the warm afternoon sun. Becca stood in his shade, staring up at him, knowing her expression was mulish.

Unfortunately, she needed his help to get loose from the dang bush!

"*Neh.* It's not for the B & B." Her response tumbled out before she'd considered her words..

"Then who is this special pie for?"

Becca reflected that she should have jumped on his assertion. Jerking her skirt again to free it from the brambles he hadn't detached from her, she muttered, "It's none of your business."

Saul gave a rusty, mocking laugh. "A special pie? Not for your job and, I'm guessing not for your *familye*. At least, Adam never said he was having special pie this night. Is the pie to be for a *Buwe* you have your eye on?"

"This is none of your business, Saul Stutztman!"

He grinned. "You should be baking me a pie, as I'm the one getting you out of this bush."

Becca glared at him. She knew better than to tell Saul her plan about Thad as he surely would have made fun of her.

Standing still, she clutched around her the little shred of composure she had as he disentangled a remaining bramble and held it aside to make a path out of the bush for her.

"There!"

She cautiously sidled past him as he held the thorny branches aside.

When Becca reached freedom, she shook out her gray skirt, hoping the thorn-holes weren't noticeable.

"Well," Saul chuckled as he stepped out of the bush, finally letting go of the brambles when he was free of it, "is the pie for me?"

"No," she snapped, "and I have no desire to tell you who I'm making it for."

"Oh, *Goedemorgen*, Becca," Chloe said, reaching up to smooth her black *Kapp*. "What are you doing here?"

They stood in the Offenthaler store a week later, and Becca stretched her mouth into a smile, wishing she'd gone to the Kreider store instead, even though it was farther away from the B & B. She didn't mind Chloe sometimes, but the girl had recently taken to bragging about the *Menner* in her life. Becca found this tiring and annoying.

14

The *Maedel* apparently didn't take to heart the importance of *Gott's* telling them to avoid pride.

Chloe definitely wasn't terrible, but she also wasn't Becca's favorite person, as the girl always acted like she was prettier and better than anyone else. Becca thought that she, herself, was far from perfect, but Chloe clearly believed she was wonderful.

"I needed some items for the breakfast muffins at the B & B for tomorrow," Becca said.

"That's right," Chloe responded in a condescending voice that made Becca want to slap her, "you are working there, aren't you? I'm saving my baking for Thad."

"*Yah?*" Becca was certain Thad's *familye* had enjoyed the pie she made them more than Chloe's dry muffins. She was sure she was the better baker, but saying so was too prideful and, she knew, wrong.

She tried to be the kind of person *Gott* directed, but it was hard some times.

Chloe's remark wouldn't have rankled as much if the girl hadn't known that Becca was acknowledged as a very *gut* baker. Chloe's own *Daed* had remarked on Becca's baking. Becca fell very short of other *Maedels* in many ways, but she could bake.

"Thad and I are going for a drive in his buggy this evening," Chloe bragged.

Before she could stop herself, Becca said, "I thought you were interested in several of the other *Buwes*."

At least, Chloe had said this. Becca wasn't sure these *Buwes* were interested in Chloe.

Preening a little, Chloe responded, "Several of them have asked me to take drives, but I like Thad more than the others, at the moment."

Poor Thad, Becca thought rebelliously.

"He's been to my *familye's Haus* several times," Chloe went on. "I believe I'll even let him drive me home after the Sing at the Hochstetlers next week."

Biting her tongue, Becca only said she was looking forward to the Sing, hoping Thad could see through Chloe. What a day she was having! Becca tried not to tap her foot. First, getting trapped in that darned blackberry bush and being found there by Saul! Now, she'd run into Chloe.

Later that afternoon, Becca flounced into the bedroom her *Bruder*, Adam, shared with Judah, their younger brother. Their younger brother was out, helping fifteen-year-old Ezra Zook round up the goats.

"Oh, I had a crazy day, Adam. I had to deal with both Chloe Nissly and Saul. That Saul Stutztman makes me so mad! The *Bisskatz*!" She dropped onto Adam's bed.

As it was almost suppertime, Adam had just washed his face and hands at the hand pump in the kitchen and was now toweling off before putting on a clean shirt.

"He's not always a skunk. What did Saul ever do to you?" Adam leaned forward to look in the mirror on the wall, running a comb through his damp hair.

"He may be your friend," she exclaimed in disgust, "but he's always picking on me! Remember, he even tried to throw me out of our own barn! Like he's the boss!"

Her brother threw her an amused look.

"Saul acts like he knows everything and never makes mistakes!"

"What happened? Did you see Saul today?"

"Yes!" Her embarrassment at being found tangled in the blackberry bush brought heat to her cheeks.

He had helped her, but he was such a jerk about it. His remarks about how she'd use the berries were uncalled for! Who she made pies for was none of his business!

Adam laughed. "You and Saul have always rubbed each other the wrong way. He's been a good friend to me, though."

From her spot on his bed, Becca frowned at her brother. "Why are the two of you friends? You're very different."

Chuckling, he said, "Thanks. I'll take that as a compliment, since you think he's a skunk and jerk."

"He is! How can you get along with someone like that? You have lots of friends and you laugh and talk easily. Saul sometimes just sits there, silent and disapproving. He has this face that shows nothing."

"A *Mann* doesn't have to talk easily to everyone to be *Gott's* child. Saul's very comfortable, once you get to know him."

"I know him too well!" Becca declared, sitting up straight on Adam's bed. "He may be nice to others—although I doubt it—but he's certainly annoying to me! I must be the only one he's not nice to.

"*Neh*, you're not."

The tone in which her *Bruder* said this perked up Becca's interest almost more than the words themselves. "What do you mean?"

"Nothing." Adam bent to dust the shoes he wore in the house.

"Brother," she crawled to the end of the bed, bracing herself on the clean, crafted footboard, "who else is Saul not friendly toward?"

"No one. I shouldn't have said anything."

"Well, you did! Tell me! Who else is Saul a skunk to?"

Adam lifted his gaze to her face for a moment, seeming to consider his response. "Some in the world are more likely to draw anger than others, that's all."

Becca's curiosity now piqued, she said in a wheedling voice. "Tell me, *Bruder*."

"If I do," Adam said slowly, "you may be more tolerant and understanding of Saul."

"Maybe." She couldn't see that happening, but she supposed it was possible.

"Saul is very protective of his *familye*—his *Mamm* and his *Geschwischder*."

She made a face. "*Yah*. Most are nice to their mother, as well as, their brothers and sisters. This doesn't necessarily make them pleasant to be around."

"Saul is more caring of his *familye* than most," Adam said after a moment.

"I know he took over their farm after his *Daed* passed, but how does this have anything to do with Saul being unfriendly to others?"

"Not others. Just one." He looked in the mirror, adjusting his jacket. "Saul can look forbidding when he first meets you, but he has a good heart."

"Who else is he unfriendly and forbidding to?" she insisted, sensing a secret in her *Bruder's* cryptic words.

Adam didn't answer immediately. After a moment, he came to stand by the foot of his bed. "He once got very angry about how an *Englischer* endangered his younger sister one time."

"Amity?" She hadn't heard about Saul's sister having any problems.

"*Neh*. Leah."

"Oh, the youngest sister?"

"*Yah*, Leah."

"She's just twenty-one," Becca stared at him. "Did some *Englischer* do something to her when she was on *rumspringa*?"

She knew the younger Stutztman sister had come back from her visit to the *Englischer* world this last spring. Had something happened to Leah when she was deciding whether to join that world or join the *Amisch* world?

"No, this was much earlier. Before their *Daed* passed," Adam responded almost without thinking.

Frowning, Becca said, "Leah must have been young, a scholar almost."

"*Yah*," Adam said, "And I'd have felt just as Saul did, if someone hurt you or any of you girls!"

"*Bruder*," she said, determination in her voice. "What did Saul do to defend his sister?"

"Mind you, he isn't proud of it. I'm sure he asked *Gott's* forgiveness."

"Maybe. Maybe not," Becca pursued, intrigued by this view of her brother's friend. "What did he do to the *Englischer*?"

"Saul didn't hurt anyone or anything near that," Adam hastened to say.

"Then it can't hurt to tell me what he did do." Becca thought her request was very reasonable. The jerk. Saul could hardly deserve all this protection. After all his teasing and torment, he didn't deserve anything from her.

Adam shrugged. "He just slashed an *Englischer's* tires, nothing more."

"What!" She squeaked in surprise. It was hard to imagine Saul doing something so—so angry and vengeful. "Why? What did the *Englischer* do to Leah? I mean, destroying another's property is—"

"Wrong?" Her brother finished. "Not acting as *Gott* would have us?"

"Something like that." Becca sat back on his bed. It was hard to imagine smug Saul doing anything like that.

"Perhaps it wasn't his finest choice," Adam conceded, "and he doesn't feel *gut* about it or what it spread around, but Leah was a child and *Englischer* almost ran over her with his big car! It's a miracle from *Gott* that the girl wasn't hurt more."

"Hurt more?" Becca thought back. She'd seen Leah at the all the services back then. She thought. At least, she couldn't remember Leah being hurt.

"*Yah*," Adam said eagerly, as if he wanted to present his friend's dilemma in the best light. "Saul is very protective of his *Mamm* and his *Geschwischder*. It's one of his best qualities. He was naturally angry about his sister. Leah was passing through a crosswalk in town, when the *Englischer* clipped her in his rush to go through it. And it wasn't as if the *Englischer* was rushing someone to the hospital or to the doctor. Adam had seen the whole thing happen, so when he saw the car parked later in town at one of the hotels, he—w ell, he knew Leah had a sprained ankle and a big bruise from the fall. He was younger and not as wise. Leah could have been killed!"

"And that's when Saul slashed the *Englischer's* tires," Becca concluded slowly, trying to absorb this new, reckless picture of him. He'd never seemed like a rebel, always looking like an upstanding *Amisch Menner*.

"Yes, you see that he's human and makes mistakes like we all do. Now maybe you will be more tolerant of him."

"And no one knows he did this?" Becca looked at her *Bruder*, a glimmer of an idea circling round in her head.

Her brother gave Becca a searching look. "*Neh*, not that I know. Saul doesn't feel *gut* about what he did. He's embarrassed, I suppose."

Narrowing her gaze, she looked unseeing into Adam's face. As if sorting out a puzzle, she said still slowly. "This is not our way, to enact revenge."

Adam shrugged. "This is why Saul's embarrassed. Why he's kept quiet about his actions."

"So, no one knows?" she asked again. She'd not heard about it, but that didn't mean others didn't. The *Amisch* were taught to respect others' privacy and not to gossip about one another.

"No, I don't think so...and you are to keep this to yourself," her *Bruder* said in a directive tone, "I only brought it up, so you'd be more understanding of Saul and see his protective side. Remember, we are directed not to gossip."

"I won't gossip," she returned, her brain still whirling. Saul! Who'd have known he had this big a secret? That he could have done something like this. He seemed so honest and so true to his beliefs, like he'd never faltered.

While her brother went on talking about his friend, Becca said little, just nodding once in a while. Knowing Saul's secret gave her a startling sense of...power. He was so mean to her that he deserved a little of his own treatment.

It was odd, really. She almost looked forward to seeing him.

"Abby. Hand me the Clear Jel," Becca held the big cream mixing bowl on her hip as she stirred its contents.

Her sister closed the oven, turning to reach into a nearby cabinet. "Is this for the strawberry pie for supper?"

"*Yah*." Becca measured the amount she needed, dumping it in the mixing bowl.

"You can definitely bake," Abby said. "Is that loaves of bread I see rising over there?"

"It is." Becca sent her a pleased smile, happy at the praise. Abby didn't hand this out too often.

"Well, don't forget that you're supposed to bake some items to take to our church services this weekend."

"Of course not." Baking was her joy. She didn't have many accomplishments, but she was a *gut* baker.

Abby, on the other hand, was good at many, many things. Her careful eye to detail and her strict attention to her tasks had them all coming out wonderfully, be these the garden she tended so well or the quilts she crafted and sold at the roadside fruit stands. She could cook well and kept their chickens in good form, as well as, canning and making jellies.

Musing as she stirred the pie filling into the crust that waited nearby, Becca thought that Abby wouldn't have stood for doing anything but the best. Becca's stitching wasn't straight or good enough to work with her older sister. She sadly had to admit to that. Overall, she wished she were more like Abby. Baking only took you so far.

Having returned to the Zook home a year ago after her husband died in an accident with another buggy, Abigail was a little older than most of the *Maedels* at church, her black *Kapp* an indicator that she'd been a *Mann's Frau* for a time. Becca had to remind herself, at times, that her sister's situation wasn't ideal.

Although pretty much everything about Abby seemed ideal. Becca sighed as she stirred.

Her older sister would probably take some well-off *Mann's* fancy and marry to have a happy *familye* of Abby's own.

"That pie filling looks yummy," their *Mamm* said as she came into the kitchen.

Becca smiled. Abby might have been perfect in every way, but she couldn't out bake Becca.

"The bread for supper is over there." She motioned with her head.

"The *Englischers* should have you bake for the B & B."

"They really should," Abigail inserted. "Your stitches may be all cockeyed when you quilt, but you can make terrific cinnamon rolls. I'd guess the *Englischer* visitors would like that."

"*Yah*," Beth Zook agreed. "And you could sell them at the farm stand with Abby's quilts."

"Do you think so?" Becca asked doubtfully. "They aren't particularly special."

"*Liebling*," her mother came to stand next to her, patting Becca's cheek, "they're cinnamon rolls and they're *gut*."

Becca leaned into her *Mamm's* quick hug.

"What's for supper?" *Grossmammie* Ruth asked Abigail, coming into the kitchen to sit at the *familye* table.

"Did we wake you with our noise?" Becca asked, catching her grandmother's eye.

"*Neh*, child. I don't always sleep well, now that I'm an old woman, but when I do, it would take more than kitchen noises to rouse me."

Becca put a dish towel over the pie and sat it in a cooler corner of the kitchen before she moved from behind the kitchen counter to her *Grossmammie's* side, kissing the withered cheek. "I believe there might be enough cream to whip and put on the pie, once Ezra and Faith do the milking."

"You are a good child, Becca." Grandmother Ruth reached up to pat her.

"It's already getting around," her *Mamm* said, "that Becca does all our baking and is very *gut* at it."

Her *Grossmammie* gave a rusty laugh. "Some *Mann* will ask her to marry him, just for that!"

Ducking her head in sudden shyness, Becca only hoped Thad would feel this way. Hoped, too, that Chloe had heard some of these compliments.

"Take my word for it," Abigail said over her shoulder as she paused in the act of feeding wood sticks to the old stove, "*Menner* want more in a wife than baking."

Downcast at her sister's caustic words, Becca forced a smile on her face. She was sure it looked wobbly as she wasn't good at hiding her feelings. Abby's claim was correct, even though it left Becca feeling as low as a worm.

"Our Becca," her *Mamm* said staunchly, "has many *gut* qualities. Baking isn't her only talent."

Becca just hoped no one asked Beth Zook to name her daughter's other skills. She was sure she had none, compared to many other *Maedels*, particularly Abby.

A week later, Saul reached up to receive another armload of corn stalks from the harvester that his brother, Abe, drove. Wearing serviceable leather gloves, Saul hefted the corn stalks onto the wagon behind himself. In front of him, young Ben drove the wagon on which Saul balanced as he reached up to receive the stalks the harvester chute sent his way.

With the season having progressed into full summer, the weather was hot and he registered that sweat trickled down his back. He was glad that his wide-brimmed hat blocked the rays from the sun beating on his head.

The three brothers pulled the corn harvest in like clockwork, having worked together as a team for the last six summers. Now that Ben had finished school, he was able to help out through this first harvesting season, while the youngest in the family, Gabe, still had to go to school one more year.

They teased *Mamm* about naming two of her sons Abe and Gabe. To which, she retorted that their given names were Abraham and Gabriel.

Saul squinted at the sweet corn in the field, the tassels shriveled and brown. He could remember clearly when his *Daed*, Zacharias, had him drive the harvester while Abe directed the horses from the wagon that carried the stalks. His father had seemed strong and invincible then.

Still in the rhythm of reaching up for the stalks from the harvester chute, a shaft of sadness went through Saul as he missed his *Daed*. His jaw hardening, he committed again to providing farms for his *Bruders*, just as Zacharias would have.

"Saul!" Ben yelled over the sound of the harvester. "Is this a *gut* speed for you? I'm trying to keep right with Abe."

"It's fine," Saul yelled, another armload of corn stalks lofting out of the harvester.

After harvesting half one field, the brothers took a break under the shade of a spreading beech tree.

His broad-brimmed straw hat on the ground next to him, he leaned back against the beech's trunk and Saul let the water his *Mamm* had sent with him run down his throat.

"Is that the field you want to buy for Ben's farm?" Sitting with his back against the tree next to him, Abe asked, taking the jug Saul handed him.

Glancing over, Saul wiped his mouth before answering, "Yah."

"It looks like it's sat fallow for several seasons," young Ben observed from where he sat in front of his two *Bruders*. "Should be very fertile."

"*Yah*," Saul said again as Abe reached the jug to Ben. "Beans grew there last, I think."

"I don't know, Saul." Abe shook his head. "I'm not sure this *Bencil* deserves a farm. Maybe he should get a job in town and work to save a while. Maybe he should work the family farm until he earns enough to buy his own place. Land is so expensive these days. He could put in some more years on *Daed's* farm and save money for some more land. I'd be happy to work this field."

Not answering this quip immediately, Saul chewed on dried apple slices that their sisters had sent for a snack.

"*Neh*! Saul helped you buy yours! That field is not part of it." Ben shot back heatedly. "I'm no more a silly child than you!"

The two older brothers laughed at this.

"Settle down, Ben," Saul recommended, tossing his leftover bread crusts at the fence line. "He's just teasing you."

"*Bencil*," Abe said softly, his shoulders shaking in laughter. "You know Saul is helping you get a farm, just as he bought mine."

"We've all worked together," Saul interjected. "Careful management yields profit. You remember *Daed* saying that."

The brothers subsided into quiet then, two leaning back against the beech tree trunk, the tree's branches providing a welcomed shade. Every so often they took drinks from the water jugs their *Schweschders* had sent with them and Ben began chewing on his own apple snacks. Earlier in the day, they'd consumed most of the lunch their sisters carefully packed, but there were still some bits left.

The road ran along edge of the field and occasional traffic passed by, some *Amisch* buggies and every now and then an *Englischer's* car.

After a while, an *Amisch* bicyclist came into view, stopping on the road to mop the sweat from under the hat he'd removed.

It was Thad Miller, Saul noticed.

Thad looked up and saw the brothers, taking a break under the spreading tree. He waved his hat at them, pushing his bicycle into the ditch that ran beside the lane. "*Hallo* there!"

Although he was younger than Saul and older than the other two *Bruders*, all three knew Thad.

"You're taking a break from early harvesting the sweet corn field?" Thad braced one foot on the bottom rung, vaulting himself over wooden fence that ran along the edge of the field.

"Is this one of the fields bought for your farm, Abe?"

"*Neh*. Mine's set up. I'll just need a barn and a house built on it. This one is for Ben," Abe answered, his lack of inflection not unlike Saul's.

Thad nodded. "You're certainly fortunate. My *familye* can't afford to buy all us boys our own farms. These are so expensive now, that most my *Geschwischder* are finding jobs in town. Some are working on the bigger corporate farms. I'm fortunate to be able to work at the feedstore with my older brothers."

25

"This is what many must do now. Find jobs in town," Saul commented. "I've heard that Jakob Mueller is doing blacksmithing in town with *Englischer* tourists watching."

"*Yah*," Thad said, "my *Bruder* said Jakob is able to charge by the head and the tourists crowd into his forge to watch him."

"He must be making a *gut* living," Ben interjected, lobbing the last of his bread crusts into the field as Saul had.

Seeing his young brother do this, Saul felt an amused tug at the corner of his mouth.

"Hey!" Thad piped up. "I think Becca Zook should go into the baking business. Maybe I should talk to her about this."

All urge to smile left Saul at the mention of his friend's *Schweschder*. She could be annoying, at times, but he saw himself as Adam's substitute in protecting Becca.

"She made a very *gut* blackberry pie for my *familye*. It was much better than most."

"A blackberry pie?" Saul echoed, remembering getting Becca loose from the thorns in that blackberry bush.

"As I said, it was better than most pies I've tasted." The subject of this dessert brought a greater animation to Thad's face. "Becca was very kind to bring us such a tasty treat."

Saul stared at him, putting two and two together—Becca in the blackberry bush and her generosity toward Thad Miller and his *familye*.

Thad. Becca was…was interested in Thad.

His next thought was that Adam's sister could do better.

Thad was a nice enough *Mann*, but Becca's baking alone would earn her plenty of *Menner*. In his opinion, the *Maedel's* blackberry pie was wasted on Thad.

What was she thinking?

CHAPTER THREE

A week later, Becca climbed out of the riverbed, struggling to pull her wet skirts free of the sluggish water. Intentional swimming was a lot of fun—this was not.

Above her spread lacy boughs of an old oak while several small red maples flamed on the banks next to the brook.

As if taunting her, the fallen tree that spread across the water sat to her left.

Dumm tree.

She felt like such an idiot.

What a foolish situation!

Hearing loud male laughter, Becca stiffened.

No, no! she thought. Some *Mann* must have seen her topple into the stream.

She'd crossed this small river many times, but never here. On this stupid log! She'd tried to walk across it so carefully!

Her black *Kapp* plastered to her wet head, rivulets trickled down her flaming neck as she bent—deeply embarrassed—to draw her skirts together to wring out as much water as she could.

The laughter continued and, as it grew closer, the mocking sound became strangely familiar to her.

Having straightened and dropped her dripping skirt, Becca felt her blush deepening till her face felt it was burning.

Saul. Again, Saul had found her in a silly situation.

Keeping her head bent as she fruitlessly tried to fluff her dripping gray skirt, she heard the crunch of footsteps as he came across the creek's rocky shoreline.

She'd have wished her observer could have been anyone besides Saul.

"Why, if it isn't *Maedel* Zook," he said, a big smile spreading across his face. His very stance was mocking.

"Don't mess with me now, Saul," she said angrily. "I'm not in the mood."

"This surprises me," he responded, the annoying laughter still in his voice. "You look very cool and comfortable."

"It's clear," she responded in a waspish voice, "that you've never been in a dripping wet dress because it's definitely not comfortable."

"You're right, *Maedel*." His shoulders shook a little. "I've not been in a dress, at all."

"Why are you even here?" Still trying to shake out her dripping skirt, she shot him a look.

"Just making my way back home," he said, shifting his broad-brimmed hat back further on his head.

"This stream isn't by your *Haus*," she muttered, upset with herself for letting him, of all people, find her like this.

"*Neh*, but my *Bruder*, Abraham's, farm lies just down the road here."

"I didn't know Abe had a farm already." Becca still couldn't bring herself to look at him directly.

"Well, he does." Saul didn't elaborate.

She knew, from remarks her own brother had dropped, that Saul was helping his younger brothers buy up property hereabout. Bragging about *gut* deeds wasn't their way, but his reticence made it seem like Saul had nothing to do with Abe getting a farm. Becca knew these were hard to come by.

She still didn't think well of him, though. His laughter at her expense made that almost impossible.

Irritating, not-so-good Saul! He deserved to be taken down a peg or two.

"Ouch!" Becca stuck her pierced thumb in her mouth, tasting salty blood. "I'll never make anything as good as your quilts, Abby."

"It just takes practice," her older sister said calmly. "You're always in too much of a hurry."

"Maybe," Becca said glumly, "but even Naomi and Faith's are better than mine. And quilts bring in such *gut* money!"

It stung that their two youngest sisters were better quilters than she. "It's understandable that Eve's better."

She mentioned her just-older sister. "Eve's been doing it longer."

"At least, Adam and our *Bruder's* aren't better," Abby responded, humor threading through her words."

"I bet they would be," Becca said gloomily, "if they weren't busy on the farm."

Abby chuckled, glancing over at Becca's work. "It's *gut* there's some red in this one as you're pricking your fingers so much."

Her grandmother, who'd been working in the nearby kitchen, came over then and reached down to give Becca a hug. "I'm sure no one could do better at your work at the B & B."

Becca flushed. No one had a better *Grossmammi* than hers. She gave a squeeze to the arm her grandmother had thrown over her shoulders. "Thank you, Grandma Ruth. I love you."

"I love you, too, *Liebling*. You're worth so much more than you think."

"Of course, she is," Abigail said in a serene voice. "Maybe not as a quilter, but very much as God's creation."

"I wish He'd created me as a good quilter." The soft coverings were not only a staple in *Amisch* homes, but were highly sought after by *Englischers* and therefore brought in *gut* money.

Grandmother Ruth kissed her on the temple. "*Gott* gives us the talents He knows are best. Be thankful."

"He does," Abigail agreed.

"And you make wonderful baked goods," her *Grossmammie* reminded her before heading back toward the kitchen. "These bring in *gut* money, too."

"I am thankful," Becca responded ruefully, "I just wish I could quilt, as well. Abby does both well. Abby does everything well."

"No one does everything well," Abigail said, her mouth tightening. "You know this."

"*Yah.*" Becca ducked her head again, trying to make her stitches neater, while keeping her thoughts to herself for once. It certainly seemed like Abby did everything well. Not even their just-older sister, Eve, was as cool and capable as Abigail.

Two days later, Saul followed Adam into the kitchen, the door slamming behind them.

"Hey, sis." Adam loped past her toward the staircase, "Did Noah bring my hat in from the barn?"

"Stop that!" Becca slapped at Saul's hand as she saw that he'd snuck a piece of the freshly-baked bread that was cooling on racks to the side.

"What?" she turned to catch Adam's question.

"Noah was to bring my straw hat in from the barn after he borrowed it from me yesterday. Did he leave it in my room as he promised? I want to wear it in the fields this afternoon."

"Stop that!" She slapped a floury hand at Saul, raising her voice as he grinned at her, taking another piece of bread. "I don't know, Adam. I think Noah was in here earlier."

"Can't you see, Adam," Saul asked in a mocking voice, "that Becca's baking and is paying no attention to anything else?"

The two *Menner* had obviously cooled themselves at the water pump outside, droplets leaving marks over Saul's shirt, the sleeves of which were rolled up to his forearms, mingling with the dark hair there.

"I'll be right down," Adam promised his friend, continuing up the stairs.

"Abby brought you all a very *gut* lunch not two hours ago," Becca said irritably to Saul. "I don't see why you need to sneak food now."

"I'm hungry. Haven't you heard that hard work makes a *Mann* hungry? Besides it smells wonderful and I can't help myself. I'm a growing boy," Saul retorted, taking yet a third slice out of the loaf.

"I didn't bake the bread for you to eat," she said in a snide tone. He annoyed her with the taunting smile on his face.

"No?" Saul responded. "You probably made it for Thad."

"*Neh.*" Becca felt heat crawl up her cheeks. "I can't imagine why you'd think it was for anyone other than my *familye*."

"No? Is that a blackberry pie for Thad that you're baking now?"

"Don't be silly." Did Saul know she'd taken a blackberry pie to Thad's *familye*? She didn't see how or know how he'd guessed that she had any more interest in Thad than any of the other young *Menner*.

"Been in any blackberry bushes recently?" Saul came closer, looming up beside her as he made his annoying remarks.

Becca's cheeks grew warmer. "You have no idea what you're talking about. I bake for lots of people hereabouts and even for the B & B."

"Thad told my *Bruders* and me how much he and his *familye* enjoyed your blackberry pie."

Ignoring the further heating of her cheeks, Becca ignored his comment, saying, "I also sell my baked goods at the farm stand on the road where Abby sells her quilts."

"I'm sure these bring in lots of money—the baked goods, I mean. Thad must have been glad to get that pie, seeing how it could have earned you money."

Irritated with Saul's inferences, she turned to him, wishing Adam would come back. She retorted, "What I do for Thad, or any other *Menner*, is none of your business."

"Maybe not," Saul responded, "but Thad's not the *Mann* for you. He's too cowardly and spineless."

Exasperated enough not to care about her red cheeks, Becca snapped, "You are not to decide this or to pass judgment on any *Mann*!"

"You can do better," Saul responded through a mouthful of bread, clearly unshaken by her reproof. Swallowing, he lifted his eyebrows, "Certainly you can find a better husband if he tastes your baking. This is very good bread."

"I don't care what you think," she retorted, although his compliment did make her preen a little to herself. Mindful that one was to be ashamed of having pride, she sent up a quick prayer, asking for forgiveness.

She didn't care what he thought, not even a little.

Still chewing a bite, Saul took a moment before saying, "I don't think you're right for Thad, either. Isn't he keeping company with Chloe Nissly?"

"This is none of your business!" Becca shot back angrily.

"I'm just saying that others are better choices for your *blaeckbier* pie. Have you thought of Stephen Yoder as a husband? He's a bit old, but I'd bet he'd really enjoy some pie."

"You are just a *bisskatz*! You stink like a skunk!" Becca snatched the rest of the bread from his hand.

"I don't think Chloe would do that," he said with mock reproach.

Letting loose an exasperated sigh, Becca asked in frustration, "What are you doing here? Are you not needed in the fields?"

"You cannot have been listening." Saul spun a dining room chair around to straddle it. "Adam is looking for his straw hat."

"He's had time enough to find ten hats!"

"Apparently, this one is hiding," reproached Saul. "You do not want him overheating while working. He needs a hat that will keep him cooler. What kind of sister are you?"

Feeling as though the top of her head might blow off if she didn't vent some of her steam, she asked, "Must you wait here for him? You could go out where the wind is blowing or, better yet, head out to the fields yourself! And aren't you needed on your own farm?"

"Not really and the wind is not as cool as one would think. Besides, it smells good here in the kitchen." He craned his neck, scanning the kitchen counters. "What else are you making besides bread? Is there more blackberry pie?"

"No! And I wouldn't offer you any if there was!"

Saul responded in a sad voice. "I bet you're saving it for Thad, even though he is keeping company with Chloe."

"He isn't!" Becca shot back. "At least, it's no one's business if he is."

Saul shook his head with a mournful expression, "I don't think you should be sharing pie with him, if he's keeping company with another *Maedel*. You should give pie to me, instead."

Jamming her floury hands on her hips, she declared, "I wouldn't give you pie if you were the last *Mann* alive!"

"*Yah*, you would, if only to beat Chloe to the last *Mann* alive."

"No, I wouldn't, you *pescht*. I'd stay a spinster rather than give you pie!"

"I may be a pest," he said, calmer as she grew angrier, "but you're too *schmaert* to do that if I were the last *Mann* alive."

"You don't think I'm smart," Becca said in a nasty voice. "You think I give pie to *Menner* who go out with other girls."

Saul stood from the chair he'd been straddling. "*Neh*, you just don't like to be bested...and I'll say it again, Thad doesn't deserve your blackberry pie, which is probably as good as your bread."

"I don't need you to tell me!" She snapped, his comments about Thad incensing her. "And it doesn't matter to me if you did see him with Chloe. I'm sure they have no interest in one another! Not that I care."

She might not be as perfect as Abby, but Chloe didn't make perfect quilts, either.

"Uh-huh," was his only response as he grinned before finally leaving the kitchen.

"That skunk!" Becca raged two days later. "That *Bisskatz*!"

Adam looked amused. "I know you and Saul haven't ever gotten along, but I still think you calling him a skunk is a bit much."

Shaking with rage, she yelped, "You're telling me that Saul took it upon himself to tell Thad that Chloe was a better mate for him?! That he actually told Thad that Chloe was better for him than I am? That *Schlang*!"

She and her *Bruder* sat alone in the dusky evening light, outside the big barn behind their house. Perched on the seat of a hay wagon while Adam leaned against the wagon's wheel, she thought again that she couldn't believe Saul's gall.

"*Yah*, he did say that, but calling him a snake isn't any better than saying he's a skunk. It wasn't like he said anything bad about you. I didn't think you liked Thad Miller anyway."

"Well, Saul is a snake! How dare he tell Thad who would make a better mate!"

"I thought you didn't get along with Chloe or Thad that well," Adam observed. "Didn't you tell me that Chloe's always trying to one-up you?"

"It doesn't matter if she's a *gut* friend or not," Becca retorted, angrier than she could remember being. "Saul has no right to insert his stupid opinions."

Adam cocked an eye at her. "Is Thad Miller that important to you? I didn't know…or are you trying to one-up Chloe now?"

Not wanting to think about his question that closely, Becca said with as much dignity as she could muster, "It isn't Saul's right to say who Chloe or I decide to pick as husbands. Or to tell Thad anything about making a choice of *Frau*."

She slumped in the hay wagon seat, tired of coming in second, particularly to someone like her classmate. Abby was different. She was better than anyone else. Her sister was perfect and made perfect quilts, as well as, doing pretty much everything perfectly.

She'd probably have had the most happy, perfect marriage, if her husband hadn't died in that buggy accident. Poor Abby.

"If Chloe's that good a friend—maybe I misunderstood—I'd think," Adam said, his light brown hair curling now that he'd removed his broad straw hat, "you'd be pleased that Saul recommended a *Mann* pursue her."

"It's not Saul's concern. He—we—have no right to say who others should marry." The skunk. It would serve him right, Becca thought angrily, if he had to convince Thad to marry her.

She wasn't totally sure she wanted to marry Thad, but it certainly wasn't any business of Saul's.

And Chloe—who truly wasn't much of a friend—would look green with envy when she learned that Thad was pursuing Becca.

She sat dreamily considering a moment when both Saul and Chloe realized she wasn't a silly *Maedel* to be mocked and dismissed, but a person to be respected. Chloe was just annoying, but this was no different than she'd always been and she was this way with everyone.

Saul was a different matter, the snake. As if he had any right to throw stones. Why he'd done much worse when he slashed that *Englischer's* tires—though no one knew it. The thought flashed through her mind that she knew Saul's secret. All that Adam had told her about that event made his actions understandable, but Saul acted like he was such an upstanding, blameless *Mann* who had the right to sneer at others!

As the light faded around her and Adam, she mused again that Saul wouldn't sneer at her if he was forced to pretend to court her.

He deserved to be used in this way! As much fun as he'd made of her.

She didn't know how to make him pretend to make up to her, though. Saul wasn't a *Mann* to be easily forced into anything. It wasn't as if she could twist his arm or wrestle him into doing it.

Although…. Saul did have a secret.

Becca threw Adam a sideways glance. He'd be very upset if she used his confidence against Saul…if he ever found out. Of course, she'd know if Adam ever found out as he'd certainly come angrily to her that she'd chosen to punish his friend with Adam's words.

Maybe....

She glanced at her *Bruder* again. Maybe he didn't need to find out. She could, she supposed, make it a part of her—her arm twisting—that Saul tell no one, not even Adam. Especially not Adam.

Or she'd make sure the church elders knew Saul's secret.

Not that it was likely to come to that, Becca said hastily to herself. Nothing had to be made public if Saul just took his medicine without complaint. And it wasn't like she would ask him to actually marry her.

He deserved this!

She could get her revenge without doing any real harm. Becca wasn't even convinced that she wanted to marry Thad, and Saul—and Chloe—could only benefit from being taken down a peg or two.

The more she thought about it, the better the idea seemed. No one would be hurt. In fact, all involved could actually benefit. This idea could work, she thought, glad that the evening shadows had begun to fall and her brother couldn't see her too-expressive face.

"It's getting dark," Adam said. "We should probably head in for dinner. *Mamm* and the other girls might need some help."

"Okay," Becca said, slipping down from the hay wagon with such a feeling of saintly satisfaction that Adam must have remarked on it, if the darkness hadn't hidden the smile on her face.

She was convinced that she'd hit on the very idea she needed to pursue.

"*Hallo*, Saul," Becca said pleasantly the next morning.

Saul stared at her a moment, surprised both to see Becca sitting on the bench outside the Oberholtzer feedstore so early and surprised that she'd greeted him so agreeably. In fact, she looked very pretty in the early morning light, smiling at him in a way he hadn't seen before.

Two thoughts hit him at once—initially, that he could get used to that pleasant smile and, at the same time, he wondered what was up. Had Thad Oberholtzer complimented her baking or asked Becca to drive out with him?

"Goedemorgen." Pausing with one foot on the feedstore porch, he hesitated. Neither possibility was good news, but Thad could have done either. He wasn't the sharpest pitchfork in the barn. Even though Saul had recommended Thad pursue Chloe, he may have decided Becca was better for him. The boy didn't know what was best for himself, which certainly wasn't a *schmaert* girl like Becca. She might be a pain sometimes, but she wasn't dumb.

"Good morning," she returned, getting up from the bench. "Perhaps we could talk a moment before you go into the feedstore?"

She glanced at a *Mann* walking past them into the store. "Somewhere less public?"

It might have been Saul's imagination, but it seemed like an odd request and he thought Becca looked a little too pleased with herself.

"What can we have to discuss," he asked suspiciously, "that would need a less public location?"

"Just things," she responded, still smiling. "I'm only thinking of your best interest. You'd definitely prefer this not to be overheard."

Saul sighed in frustration, irritated. He'd suspected she was up to no good, but even Thad's compliment wouldn't make her say this. Had blackberry pie made Thad propose? No, Saul's rational mind said calmly. Why would he prefer that not be overheard?

He was considering telling Becca that he had nothing he didn't want overheard when she said, "Perhaps we could go down to where your buggy is parked? I doubt many will hear us over there."

Curious what the scamp was up to, Saul chuckled finally, saying, "Okay."

He followed her to the far side of the feed store parking area and they stood by his buggy as he said, "So, what's all this about Becca?"

Lifting her chin, a glimmer of a smile crossed her expressive face and she said triumphantly, "I have a proposition for you, Saul."

Just for a moment, it crossed his mind that Becca was going to…ask him to drive out with her? *Neh*. That seemed unlikely.

Not that it was an unpleasant possibility.

"What?"

At his blunt question, her smile dimmed and she snapped, "I want you to court with me and act like you want to marry me." Becca didn't sound the least like a *Maedel* who was interested in a *Mann*.

"Why?" Saul demanded, more and more intrigued. "Why would I do that?"

"Because that would keep me," she was back to her superior smile, "from telling everyone your secret?"

"What secret?"

"Why, that you slashed an *Englischer's* car tires."

Saul stared at her for a moment.

He'd almost forgotten that moment, it had been so many years ago.

Saul truly regretted his foolish actions. He'd been young and had acted when under powerful emotions. To have this thrown back in his face when the act had been unknown by most, stung some, but less than he'd expected. He assuredly didn't like the idea of all their neighbors knowing his sin, but he'd lived for years with the certainty that *Gott* knew his stupid behavior.

Silence fell between them, Saul's gaze brooding on her as a bird twittered high in the tree above them, evidently enjoying the cool morning air.

Saul didn't ask how Becca had come to learn of this. He knew, as he'd only spoken about it to his bishop and to Adam, Becca's brother. It must have slipped out of Adam.

"What are you asking? You want me to help you make Thad jealous? You want to marry Thad?"

"Maybe. I haven't decided. Right now, I just hate Chloe thinking she can have any *Mann* she wants."

Slowly, he said, "So, this is about besting Chloe?"

"Yes! I don't know." Becca frowned, fiddling with her *Kapp* strings. "I mostly just think Thad deserves better."

"You're protecting Thad?" Saul said, not bothering to keep the derision out of his voice.

"I guess. Maybe," she lifted her chin a little. "My reasons aren't your concern, though. You need to think about your own welfare."

Saul didn't think *Gott* had decreed that they should each think only about their own interests, but he didn't point that out to Becca.

Instead, he asked, "If I don't do as you ask, what will you do?"

He'd asked *Gott* for forgiveness for his actions years ago. He'd even tried to find the *Englischer* to replace the *Mann's* tires. Becca's proposition, however, intrigued him. She interested him, the scamp. He didn't think the Bishop would censor him now, but Saul looked into the bright, blue eyes of his best friend's sister and pondered that maybe he should block her pursuit of Thad Oberholtzer.

Thad just wasn't the *Mann* for Becca, weakling that he was. Saul knew Adam would agree.

When he didn't say anything for a minute, she threatened, "I won't say anything for a week or so, but I want your answer pretty quickly."

CHAPTER FOUR

A day later, Becca navigating the streets from the dry cleaners to the B & B, lost in her own thoughts. On her way to the cleaners with an armload of B & B drapes that hadn't been washed properly, she'd crossed paths with Thad and his younger *Bruder*.

They'd done little more than wave *Hallo*, but that didn't mean anything. Not really.

She couldn't say Thad made her heart beat faster, but he was a nice *Mann* who certainly deserved better than Chloe.

Becca made a face at no one in particular. Chloe was annoying.

Stopping at a corner to let the traffic light change before crossing, she spied Saul in the Kreider's store parking lot. She'd had no idea she'd see him there, so his presence startled her and she found herself getting angry.

He'd just placed a bucket of water down for his buggy horse, the buggy pulled to a stop in the parking area in front of the store. Becca found herself marching across to him.

Stopping in front of him, she demanded, "Are you taking me seriously?"

"What do you mean?" Saul's deadpan expression was shaded by his broad hat.

"It occurs to me," she said heatedly, "that you might have convinced yourself that I wasn't serious. I am very serious."

For some reason, the thought of him dismissing her so easily rankled!

"Are you?" he responded, a hint of humor in his words.

"Yes!" she said impatiently. "Very, very. Are you going to do as I directed?"

Saul bent to shift a bucket of feed under the buggy horse's nose. He responded finally, "I'm considering the situation. This is a big matter. You've threatened me with exposure of something very personal and private."

He glanced at her. "Why would you think I'm not taking you seriously?"

Becca glared at him with suspicion, all the while reminding herself that she'd gotten used to being seen as a flighty, silly *Maedel*. At least, if it didn't have to do with baking.

His question shouldn't have made her feel silly, but it did and this left her more angry.

She didn't answer his question. "Well, you should! You'd better take me seriously!"

"Church service is this next Sunday," he said calmly. "I'll make my decision by then. Is that not soon enough? Besides, don't you want everyone to see me making up to you? If I decide, I'll do it then. My behavior can't seem to be just for Thad or he might get suspicious. Unless, you think he's the kind of *Mann* who wouldn't get suspicious."

"No. No, that's a *gut* idea. It should be where everyone can see." She squinted at him skeptically. "If you make the right choice."

"Frankly, Thad doesn't seem to me like he thinks a lot," Saul continued as if she hadn't spoken, "but I'm just looking at it from your point of view."

"He does, too, think a lot. You're just not being fair to Thad," she defended. She was far from ready to marry anyone and she certainly hadn't decided she wanted to marry Thad, but Saul had no reason to consider Thad a lightweight.

At least, she didn't think so. Anyway, Saul annoyed her a lot more than Chloe.

She'd decided to get Thad to pursue her because she just really didn't want Chloe to think she only had to crook her finger at a *Mann*.

"You're to act like you really want to be with me." Becca wasn't sure why she felt the need to spell this out to Saul. "No teasing or acting like you're too good for any girl."

"I don't think I'm too good for any girl," Saul said mildly. "If I decide to go along with your plan, I'll make it look *gut*."

At least, his tone seemed mild to Becca, which made her squint at him suspiciously. "I don't believe you. You do think you're too good for any girl."

He sighed. "I don't."

"Then why haven't you ever made up to any *Maedel*?" she demanded.

"Because I haven't wanted to," Saul returned calmly. "I'll give you my answer at services. Now, is that all? I need to get a few things for my *Mamm* from the store."

She looked at him a minute. Becca was starting to feel hopeful. Maybe he would help her. She hoped so, because she really didn't want to tell his secret, fool that she was. "All right. Sunday, then."

Starting to walk away, she turned back, "If you decide to go along with this, when are you coming by the *Haus* after services? You'll have to do that if Adam is to believe this."

Saul sighed again, like she was tiresome. "I haven't yet decided what I'm going to do."

"But just in case you do decide to—to keep your actions away from others' ears, when would you come by the *Haus*?" She was more anxious about convincing her brother than she wanted Saul to see. Adam was no fool.

"I don't know and I haven't made up my mind."

Becca watched as he turned to go into the store. She couldn't help wondering what Saul would choose, but pushing him more, at the moment, didn't seem like a good plan.

Several days later, Becca sat beside sandy-haired Thad at the meal after the sermon at the Altorfer *Haus,* smiling at him and doing her best to look interested.

Around them, others sat eating at different tables while children scampered through the crowds, playing after finishing their meals.

Congratulating herself for finding a seat next to Thad after his table had cleared, Becca smiled at him. Thad was a nice enough *Buwe* and she knew he was likely to be given a least part ownership of his father's feedstore, which made him a good catch.

Not that this mattered, but as her sister, Abby, had said, a girl needed to think about her future.

Conversations from those at nearby tables rising and falling around them, Becca settled into her bench seat, knowing this was a good time to act on her plan to get Thad's interest.

Trying not to look as awkward and artificial as she felt, Becca widened her smile, blinking at him the way she'd seen other *Maedels* do with boys. She'd never specifically tried to engage a *Mann's* interest before, having always been happy to join groups of friends.

"What are you doing these days?" It wasn't the most brilliant opening to a conversation, but she thought she offered it in a matter-of-fact, casual way. Not like a *Maedel* on a man hunt or anything.

Thad chewed for a moment before answering.

"My *Daed* has my *Bruders* and I working with him in the feedstore. He's stocking feed corn there this year, but he's talked of putting in different kinds of wheat and barley feed next." He took another bite of the beet salad on his plate.

"That's *gut.*" She blinked inanely a number of times.

Saul probably didn't think much of Thad because he didn't seem like he'd set up a business of his own. Not like Saul, Thad was more of a go-along kind of *Mann.*

That would certainly be more comfortable.

She smiled at him brightly, saying, "I'm sure working in the feedstore is interesting."

"It is," Thad responded before falling silent again.

"Your brothers are working with you?" Becca plowed ahead.

"They are. Several of them, anyway. The others found jobs in town."

"What are you doing?" She really wasn't all that interested, but they had to talk about something.

"Feedstore stuff, mostly. You know, stocking feed and things."

"Oh." Fatigue at keeping the conversation settling over her, Becca was almost—but not totally—glad to notice Chloe coming their way. She couldn't help assuming an unsmiling expression. Naturally, Chloe would have noticed them talking alone.

"*Hallo*! I'm so glad you found a table."

"*Hallo*," she offered as Chloe got closer.

Becca felt her mouth quirk up on one side at the implication that either of them were looking for a table for them all to share.

The other *Maedel* scooched her way onto the table bench between Becca and Thad. Becca wryly moved over as the other girl settled herself.

"What are you, two, talking about?" Chloe asked, throwing Thad what looked to Becca like a provocative glance.

"Nothing much," he replied around his mouthful of beet salad.

"I'm so glad then!" Chloe threw her a triumphant smile. "I'm not interrupting."

"*Neh*. Not at all." Seeming unruffled by having his private time with Becca interrupted, Thad took another bite from his plate. He didn't actually look distressed in the least at Chloe's intrusion and that just made Becca more determined to snare his interest. Jerk that he was.

Chloe wasn't winning this one. Thad didn't know the danger he faced.

"Did you make this beet salad?" he asked, clearly enamored of his plate.

"*Neh*, but I'll get the recipe, if you like it!" Chloe simpered at him.

Thad didn't appear to notice, continuing to eat, but Becca began to wonder if he just didn't notice much.

As Chloe began chattering about the Sing planned at her *Haus* after the next Sunday service, Becca gloomily wondered briefly if Thad was worth saving from the other girl's devices.

"Of course," the other girl smiled significantly, "Joseph Bacher, Ezekiel Detweiler and Reuben Gindelsberger   have all said they'll be there. They've all asked for seats near me."

She fluttered her eyelashes in a significant assumption of modesty after listing several *Menner* who'd been in school with them.

"Well, I have a suitor who wants to sit by me, as well," announced Becca loudly, galled by Chloe's nauseating claim.

Chloe gave a tinkling laugh. "Really? You've not said who he is? Do you not want to claim him?"

"*Neh*," Becca said with sweetness, "as we are recommended to be plain and unassuming."

Looking irritated by this very accurate statement, Chloe said, "I don't believe anyone has asked to sit by you."

"*Yah!*" Becca responded, feeling both embarrassed and dismayed as a flush climbed up her cheeks. "A *Mann* has, too."

She had several *Menner* friends, but she didn't think of them, at the moment.

"I don't believe you," Chloe scoffed, clearly glad to have the scene play out in front of Thad.

Leaning unseen against a nearby tree, Saul was close enough to the trio to hear their interchange. No expression crossed his face as he absorbed it all. Chloe was being a *Bisskatz*...and, of course, Thad sat there, looking as clueless as he was.

Seeing Becca, all red-faced and humiliated, made Saul's decision for him. She was annoying and sometimes ridiculous, but she certainly didn't deserve this.

Straightening from the tree, Saul sauntered forward, walking over to the table where the three sat.

"*Hallo*." He smiled significantly at Becca. "Is this seat taken?"

Without waiting for an answer, he slid on the bench next to her.

Obviously startled by his arrival at her side, Becca stammered a denial.

"*Hallo*," he greeted the other two, receiving a smile and a nod from Thad, who looked surprised and not happy at Saul's sudden appearance.

Chloe said nothing, only staring at him

"I saw you in church," he said pleasantly to Becca, "but I'm sure you didn't see me as my seat was behind big Silas Baer."

He named a particularly husky farmer they knew.

She stared at him with big eyes, not seeming to believe what she was seeing.

Not waiting for Becca to recover from her shock, Saul asked pleasantly, "Are you coming to the Sing next week?"

"*Yah*. I-I am," she stammered.

"May I take you home in my buggy?" he asked, his look infusing significance to the question.

Becca looked even more startled then. He hoped she caught on soon, so this worked.

"Yes, I sup—" She stopped short when Saul turned then to give her a significant glance. Becca suddenly seemed to get then what he was doing. "Oh, *yah*. Yes. Yes, Saul. I'd like that."

Her response seemed less spontaneous than was helpful, but still in the right direction.

All through their interchange, Chloe was silent.

Saul smiled at her, intending to confirm what she'd doubted and then turned to give Becca his best interested look. He could fake interest very well, when he wanted.

"*Gut*." Saul said with warmth. "I wasn't coming if you wouldn't be there."

"That was great!" Becca gave a happy little jig as the two walked away from the table where Chloe still sat with Thad, rejoicing, "We destroyed her!"

He didn't bother to point out the problems with this declaration—for which she was grateful—Saul just said, "Hush. They'll hear you."

Knowing he was right, she lowered her voice, saying, "I know *Gott* wants us to love others, but you have to admit Chloe makes this difficult!"

"She does seem a little proud of herself," Saul said in a low tone, no inflection in his voice.

Becca noted that as the two rounded the corner of the Altorfer *Haus*, the tall, solid *Mann* beside her gave no evidence of being moved by their recent conversation with a *Maedel* she'd come to see as her rival.

Certainly, Chloe was her rival for Thad's interest.

"You were great!" she jigged again. "She didn't believe me and you made her eat her words!"

Saul said nothing, just looking at her with a weary gaze.

"You must have decided to help me!" Becca heard herself and said more sternly, "You must have known I would do as I said."

"Maybe." Looking at her expressionlessly, he said, "I think starting with church services from this point forward is the best, don't you? Adam will be sure to suspect something if I just start mooning over you at your house. I'll eat beside you at the next sermon and, of course, drive you home from the Sing."

"Okay." Becca examined his expression with suspicion. He sounded like this game was of his design and she couldn't believe he'd given thought to how to make her threats work for them both. Why was he going along with this?

Becca studied Saul. He didn't seem like he was shivering with fear that she might tell his secret. As a matter of fact, now that she thought of it, Saul didn't seem like the kind of *Mann* who could be easily scared.

"I don't want your *Bruder*," Saul explained in his calm voice, "to think something is strange about this. I mean, he'll still think it, but he'll probably just conclude that I've lost my mind. People do all sorts of strange things when it comes to picking someone to court."

"Oh." She ducked her head, feeling some of the wind taken out of her sails at this. "Why are you going along with this?"

He looked at her a long moment.

"It'll be more convincing, too," Saul continued, seeming unaware of her lessened enthusiasm, "if I ask Adam some questions, like I'm starting to have interest in you. Like whether you're courting or driving out with anyone."

"Why?"

Saul shot her his sarcastic smile. "You've threatened me, remember? You'll talk about my having slashed the *Englischer's* times, otherwise."

"Oh," she said again.

"Remember," Saul said, "if this is to keep my secret a secret, it must be convincing."

She supposed his plan was logical, but he seemed to be taking her threat better than she would have expected.

"Okay."

"And if I help you in this, you'll not come back to the matter again? You won't hold this over me?"

Her smile widened at his agreement. "I won't. I promise, but let's be clear. You are not to say anything to Adam about our plan—never, ever—and you are to act like you are completely smitten with me."

Saul looked at her for a moment. "You don't think Adam will say anything to me about this?" he asked, a glimmer skepticism in his voice.

"If he does," Becca responded in an optimistic tone, "you just tell him that I've always seemed... lively and—and fun."

Her voice turned menacing and she scowled at him. "It's in your best interest to convince him that you find me charming."

Saul grinned. "You sound anything but charming at the moment."

Two weeks later, the light outside was fading as the Sing at the Huber *Haus* desserts were served on a long table beside them.

"Why are you so nervous?" *Grossmammie* Ruth asked, patting Becca's hand as they sat in chairs at the side of the living area.

Becca didn't know what to say. Saul would be here and she knew he'd already put her plan in action with Adam. However, this was the first time others would see them together. The first time others would see Saul act interested in her. She drew in a breath at the thought.

The service that morning didn't count, really, as he hadn't sat next to her during the sermon, but had just eaten with her for the lunch. While this might have been noted and remarked on privately, she doubted his being at her side then had raised any eyebrows. Others probably thought he'd sat there because it was the only seat.

Tonight would be different, though. Tonight, they really had to sell it.

She hoped she could act her part. Up till now, she'd been so focused on getting Saul to do this, she hadn't considered fully that she, too, would have to pretend interest. In him. She'd always known Saul to be Adam's friend, a kind of irritated, irritating *Mann*.

She actually didn't dislike Saul.

Now, she had to act flattered at his pretended focus. The thought was unsettling. Not distasteful, but unsettling.

"It's nothing, *Grossmammie*," she evaded. "I'm just excited from the games earlier, that's all."

"I watched you all play volleyball," her grandmother said. "You were very *gut*. Even against the boys, you did well."

"*Denki, Grossmammie*," Becca responded in a depressed voice. She didn't know why she felt so dejected, though, it did occur to her that it would be nice to have a *Buwe* do all the things Saul had been pressured into. Do them for real.

"I also noticed that Saul Stutzman both stood beside you for the volleyball game and sat beside you at the singing."

Becca felt herself blushing. "Did he?"

"*Yah*." Her *Grossmammie* leaned forward to again pat her hand. "He's a nice *Mann*, Saul. I don't think I've ever seen him so attentive to a *Maedel*."

For some reason, she couldn't claim this, even though making Thad jealous by Saul's evident pursuit was the goal.

Still flushed, she demurred, "I don't think he's—that way—to me. His position in playing volleyball and where he sat during the singing was just a coincidence."

At that very moment, Saul approached them with two plates in his hands. "*Goedenavond, Frau* Zook. Would you like these goodies?"

"*Denki*, Saul. Old women like me appreciate food being brought to us."

He smiled, then turned to hand the other plate to Becca. "For you."

Seeing him being...friendly and attentive was...strange. Particularly when he directed this toward her. In a strangled voice, she said, "*Denki*."

"Of course." He sat down in the seat next to her as if she'd been saving it for him. "That was a good game of volleyball. You played very well."

Becca knew she was a decent player. That was easy compared to sitting here with him. She knew she was to appear—at least to Chloe and Thad—that she was on the receiving end of Saul's attentions. This had been her idea, but she'd never gotten to the place of envisioning Saul actually acting interested in her. She suddenly didn't know how to act.

"Did you enjoy the game?" he asked, seeming amused by her awkwardness.

"I did." She forced herself to smile. "Did you?"

"I did, as well. You were surprisingly a good *Maedel* to play the game with."

Surprised by this comment, she glanced up at him. She was aware, as well, that her *Grossmammie* looked over in surprise.

Saul grinned at her.

"I'm glad I didn't get in your way," she responded in a dry voice. This was the Saul she knew. Annoying and teasing her.

"You didn't." He snared a cookie from her plate. "Can I drive you home in my buggy?"

"Why would you want to?" she snapped.

He smiled again, this time a little warmer. A smile she hadn't seen before. Becca felt a little hiccup in her heart that surprised her.

"Because I do want to, that's all. Can I drive you?"

"Yes. *Yah*, I guess," she stammered, bewildered by his turn from teasing to…whatever this was.

For the next half hour, while others ate and visited around them, Saul stayed at her side. A smiling, companionable Saul. He bent his head to her to hear her comments, got a few more goodies for her *Grossmammie* and acted in general like he…he liked Becca.

He did just as she'd ordered. It shouldn't have surprised her or caught her off guard, but it did. This was a very different Saul than she'd ever seen. He seemed to like her in reality.

She'd never known he was such a *gut* actor.

An hour later, Becca sat beside him in his buggy—apparently one of several he owned—and she found herself unable to think of anything to say. The silence seemed to ripple under her skin and she reflected that riding with him like this was very strange.

"It occurs to me," Saul commented "that I need to know more about you to carry this off."

She turned to look at him.

Wearing his broad brimmed hat despite the sun having set a while back, she couldn't see his dark, close-cut hair, but his decided chin was visible, even in the dim light.

"How do you think it went?"

Saul's deep voice startled her out of her thoughts.

"I don't know," Becca responded. "Okay, I guess."

There was no way to tell him that his behavior felt totally odd to her.

"At least, we gave a few people something to think about," he said with satisfaction in his voice.

In the dark buggy, she couldn't see his face clearly and was glad he probably couldn't see hers. She was sure she looked as unsettled as she felt. It was always her frustration that her feelings were visible on her face.

Becca cleared her throat before asking, "When do you think you'll talk to Adam?"

In the dim light, she saw Saul turn to look at her. "I'll probably see him in the next few days. I thought I'd ask him a few questions about you then."

"What kind of questions?" It might not have been good to ask this, but she couldn't help wondering.

Saul didn't respond right away and she could imagine the pondering look on his face. "I'll probably mention what a pest you can be."

Exhaling in exasperation, she said, "Well, that should convince him that you have an interest in me."

She saw Saul's hat turned toward her again. "I didn't say I'd stop there. I'll probably add that, even though you're a pest, you're kind of cute. In an annoying way."

Becca made a frustrated sound in her throat.

"Listen, *Maedel*," Saul said, strained patience in his voice, "you want this to be believable, don't you?"

"*Yah*, I suppose so," she admitted, still exasperated even though what he said made sense.

"Then, I can't make this turn too quickly," he commented, adding, "Adam's *schmaert*. He'd see through your game right away."

Stung, she shot back, "This isn't a game! I'm very serious, Saul."

She was tired of being treated like a child!

He turned toward her again. "You're this interested in Thad?"

"No! Well, I don't know." Becca fell silent for a few minutes, trying to think how to express the emotions roiling in her chest. "Chloe always wins! She always gets what she wants. You remember how she was in school. You wouldn't stand never winning, either! And my *Schweschder*, Abby, is just perfect. Even Dinah doesn't mess up like I do and she's only a year older. She's found a boy she wants to marry and she knows her path. I'm still out here wandering along without direction or boy. I mean, I have lots of *Buwes* who like my baking and who are perfectly happy to drive me home from Sings, but that's where it stops."

Silent during her heated words, Saul didn't respond immediately when she fell silent. When he did respond in his deep calm way, he said, "What makes you think Abby's perfect? We are none of us perfect."

"Yeah, well," she said glumly, "Abby's pretty close. You should see her tiny stitches on the quilts she makes and she cans beets better than anyone."

Saul's rusty laugh made her turn and look at him with suspicion.

All he said was, "*Menner* don't care about the stitches on quilts or even canned beets, when they choose a *Maedel* to marry."

"Maybe not," she said, her mood lifting a little, "but those are still important things."

"Definitely, if you like beets."

"Or staying warm under a quilt."

Snorting, he said, "Even a quilt with crooked stitches will keep you warm."

"*Yah*, but they don't sell as well to *Englischers*."

"*Englischers* buy other things, like bread and cakes."

She couldn't argue with this. "I make better bread than Chloe or Abby."

"You make better bread than most, but you don't need to brag about it. The bread speaks for itself."

She felt, rather than saw, him turn toward her, "So, you want to make Thad want to marry you, but you're not sure you want to marry him? This is just to best Chloe?"

"I don't know," Becca said defensively. "I might want to marry him. Maybe."

"Seems like a lot of trouble to go through for a *Buwe* you 'might' want to marry."

"This isn't your decision," she snapped. "I've told you my reasons. You're just trying to save yourself from your own choices!"

He said nothing and she sat fuming on the buggy seat next to him.

When they arrived at her home, she hardly waited for the buggy to stop, snapping at him that she could see herself inside.

The next morning, Saul hung the heels of his shoes over the rung of the stool in front of the feedstore counter. He hoisted himself into a more comfortable position before laying his broad hat on the counter, next to the register.

"Hey, Ezekiel. How is your harvesting going?" Saul asked

His friend shrugged. "As well as can be expected. At least *Gott* has sent us dry weather."

Saul nodded before asking about the feedstore counter man. "Where's Noah?"

"Oh, he's checking on some fertilizer I asked for. Are your fields doing well?" Ezekiel returned, as the two friends hadn't talked much in a while.

Another *Mann* guffawed from the end of the counter. "Saul's such a careful, watchful farmer that his crops don't dare fail."

Letting a small smile crease his face as his friends chuckled, Saul said, "Reuben, you're correct. We'd all be *narrish* to be in this work and not be careful. Farming depends on this from us."

"It would be crazy," Ezekiel agreed, nodding. "Sometimes I think I'd be better off selling my place and finding a job in town."

"Just promise me first refusal on your land, if you decide to do this," Saul commented.

"Make sure he pays fair market value," Reuben hooted from the other end of the feedstore counter. "Saul can certainly afford it."

Saul tilted his head back, smiling ruefully as his friends ribbed him.

After a few moments, Ezekiel said, "I saw you sitting next to Becca Zook and her *Grossmammi* at the Sing last night and didn't I see you headed out to drive her home?"

"*Frau* Zook?" Reuben teased.

"*Neh*," Ezekiel responded. "Becca Zook. I think I saw you walking toward where the buggies were parked."

Reuben observed. "She seems like a nice *Maedel*, though, a married man like me doesn't notice, of course."

"Of course." Saul hid his smile.

Ezekiel nodded. "Nice looking, too. Not that this matters as much as the heart."

"It doesn't hurt," Reuben noted.

Saul noted that the feedstore worker must be having a hard time finding Ezekiel's fertilizer.

"I didn't know you were looking for a *Frau*," Reuben said.

"Don't get in a stir," Saul recommended. "I just drove the girl home."

"This is how these things get started," Reuben observed, as if speaking from experience.

Saul looked at him meditatively, pondering his words. While Saul knew himself to be fairly strong-minded and even bullheaded, at times, he didn't immediately dismiss that Becca had some charms. Not that she saw herself this way, but still, she was, in some moments, surprisingly engaging. Even when she was angry, oddly enough.

Gott knew the wrong he'd committed when slashing the *Englischer's* tires and *Gott* knew why he'd done this. Even though Saul had confessed his actions to their bishop and wasn't concerned he'd be shunned by the church and his family, he wasn't keen on having his business gossiped about. It certainly wouldn't do the church members any service to be handed a juicy tidbit, either.

For some odd reason, though, he'd begun to think that, even though she'd reiterated her threat, Becca wouldn't act on it. She just felt she needed a victory somewhere and Becca had decided to take on bragging, smug Chloe.

Becca was a good girl.

After a few minutes spent in expressionless examination of Reuben's assertion that driving a girl home from a Sing somehow started a courtship, Saul said, "I'll take my chances."

CHAPTER FIVE

A week and a half later, Becca sat next to her *Mamm* during the sermon, praying silently to *Gott* to help her know if she was doing wrong by Saul. Oddly enough, she wasn't as worried about wronging Chloe.

Jerk that he was, Saul probably deserved this. He was such a *Schmaert Mann*, at least, he thought he was.

The home in which they worshipped was hot inside, despite the open windows, and she fanned herself with a paper fan she'd brought from home. When the speakers had finished, the crowd began to surge out, Becca, her *Grossmammie* and her *Mamm* remained in their chairs, waiting for the room to clear out some.

"I've noticed," her *Mamm* said in a low voice, "that you've been spending some more time with Saul."

Becca felt herself starting to flush more than the heat could account for. Courting couples often didn't tell even their parents that they were doing this until right before marriage. Still, she felt tongue-tied and awkward in this implied lie.

Stammering, she said after a minute, "Saul's not as irritating as I've thought before."

She'd complained often enough to her *Mamm* about her *Bruder's* closest friend. She knew she couldn't now suddenly forget all that.

"He drove her home from the last sing," *Grossmammie* Ruth said with significance.

Her face flaming even more red, Becca said, "It was just a buggy ride. Nothing to get excited about."

Mamm chuckled, patting the nerveless hand on her knee. "Saul's a good *Mann*. Your *Daed* and I like him a lot."

The rustling and chattering of their friends around them suddenly ringing loud in her ears, she murmured some half-intelligible comment, chastising herself fiercely for this new complication. Her parents liked Saul.

"Your *Daed* was my brothers' friend, too."

She hadn't even considered that their charade would affect others, aside from knowing she had to silence Adam's potential suspicion.

Grossmammie, sitting on her other side, chuckled. "I remember the buggy rides your *Grossdaddi* and I took back when we started courting."

"It was just one buggy ride. Saul probably thought it was easier to ask me than another *Maedel*," Becca protested desperately.

"As this is between you, Saul and *Gott*, I have nothing more to say of the subject," *Mamm* said briskly as she rose to exit down the row.

Trailing after her, Becca sent up a prayer of forgiveness. She hated involving *Mamm* and *Daed* and *Grossmammi* in her plans. Silly plans, after all. Weren't they supposed to offer others forgiveness and grace? *Gott* certainly offered that to them.

She desperately hoped *Gott* would forgive her. This buggy seemed to be thundering forward in a way she'd never considered.

Letting herself out the B & B side door the Monday after her *Mamm's* comment, Becca walked down the drive to where Abby sat waiting in the family buggy.

While she usually enjoyed her work and welcomed each day, she hadn't been able to shake her cloudy mood since realizing how her and Saul's forced conduct affected those around them.

"I'm glad you could pick me up," she offered after greeting her *Schweschder*. "*Mamm* is glad to have you run the *familye* errands."

"I don't mind," her elder sister responded in a serene voice. "*Mamm* always has much to do. I'm very fortunate to have *Eldre* that wanted me to return home after Gabe died."

"Don't be *verrict*," Becca returned more sharply than she'd intended. "Why would they not welcome your return? You're wonderful company and very helpful, all the time."

Her older sister never set a foot wrong, even as she stitched perfectly. Abby did everything well—even her bread was pretty good—and Becca was always aware of this compared to her deeply-flawed self.

"Not all the time." Abby clicked to set the horse moving.

"*Yah*, all the time! Like helping out by running *Mamm's* errands and by picking me up. And, of course, you're here at exactly the time you said," Becca added in a gloomy voice as she settled herself on the buggy seat next to her sister.

"You didn't have to be picked up. You could have walked home," Abby pointed out calmly. "And you've done the *familye* errands many times before walking home."

Abby's responding laugh was short before she added, "I'm far from being as perfect as you imagine."

Giving her elder sister a hard stare, Becca snapped, "Don't be ridiculous. You sew perfectly. You always say the right thing. You live the most simple and plain life of anyone. Even *Mamm* and *Grossmammi* Ruth aren't as perfect as you."

Her sister's refusal to see this almost seemed patronizing.

"You married a good *Mann* and lived a good life together until he died."

Abby sighed. "Becca, you know nothing of being married. None of us are perfect."

With this, she clucked again to the buggy horse and drove on without more comment.

Everything in her sister's attitude said that the subject was closed and Becca sat beside her on the buggy seat, making no further comment. Abby always seemed serene and contained, like nothing bothered her. She always looked cool and comfortable, wisps of her hair never even escaping her *Kapp*. Next to her, Becca was always a mess. Always wearing a kitchen-stained skirt and with tendrils of her hair sneaking out to curl at her neck.

Abigail's comment was right, too. Becca knew little about being married.

A week later, Saul held the buggy reins in his hand as Becca settled into the seat next to him. Around them, the late summer air had turned a little cooler as the evening approached.

"*Denki* for taking me out driving," she said after a few minutes with what was clearly determined cheerfulness.

"It's no more than I would do," he responded in a laconic tone, noting silently that the top of her head came just to his shoulder.

They trotted along in silence for several minutes, Saul reflecting to himself that Adam's sister could be a pleasant companion when she chose.

Looking at a thicket of trees as the buggy jogged past, she mused aloud from beside him. "The autumn color will start to show soon."

Saul glanced away from the road, saying after a moment, "*Neh*. You're crazy. The heat will be with us for a month, at least."

He then fell into silence, comfortable beside her.

Lifting her brows at his terse response, she asked, "Does the buggy ride not come with conversation?"

He looked down at her, his hands still steady on the reins. "What, exactly, do you want to converse about? I believe summer comes before the cooler weather every year."

Chuckling, she rolled her blue eyes. "*Neh*? Every year?"

Casting her a sideways glance, the corner of his mouth lifting in amusement, Saul said, "I'm so sorry I'm not conversing to your liking."

"At least, you could talk about your farms or your crops. Something, anyway."

"What would you like to hear? The price of corn or beans? My plans for next spring's crops or which farms I think might come up for sale next year? The farm equipment I plan to buy?"

Becca sighed comically. "You're already thinking about what crops you'll plant next year? And what fields you might buy? Next year?"

"*Yah*. It's good to plan these things."

"You could wait until next year to think about these. Not everything needs to be planned."

Shrugging, Saul said, "Then, I might not be ready."

Becca pulled back to look up at him more fully. "You? Not ready? Your *Daed* died when you'd just left school and you've run the farm for seven—eight—years?"

"I was seventeen." Saul's response was clipped. Thinking of that particular loss was still hard.

"So, nine years," she concluded.

"Eight." He scowled at her.

Chuckling, she said, "And you think you need to decide now what to plant because you might be undecided come spring? After eight years of running farms and deciding on the best crops? Not to mention the years you worked with your *Daed* before having to handle everything."

Saul maintained his scowl despite her compliment.

Becca seemed completely unaffected by his irritation, he noted.

"Maybe."

"And you're thinking about farms that may come up for sale?"

"Farms are expensive and I need to save to buy these. Gabe will need one soon."

"I know land is costly, but isn't Gabe only thirteen? The same age as my youngest sister, Faith? Seems like you'll have some time."

"*Yah,*" he said, "and I suppose you think money to buy farms is quickly saved."

"Of course, not, but you don't have to know which farm you'll buy to save money." She peered up at him and said, "No doubt, you've already saved some."

He didn't bother responding to this, saying only, "Look, seeding crops and buying farms isn't the same as deciding which muffins you'll bake at the B & B. These things take consideration."

"You don't need to sneer at my work, just because you're consumed by yours."

She was the most infuriating brat. Becca wasn't a child, but she certainly seemed like one at moments like these.

"I didn't sneer," he responded in a long-suffering tone. "I'm just pointing out that we have reason to see things differently."

Becca turned back to look at the road ahead. "We certainly do see things differently."

Needled by her tone, he continued to defend. "And planning crops just makes sense. Different plants need different things in the soil."

"Yes, but these things are usually plowed into the dirt weeks before planting, not months," she pointed out, farmer's daughter that she was.

Saul almost snapped back that he knew better than she did when to amend the soil, but he decided not to dignify her remark.

After a moment, she commented in a cheerful, musing tone, "I do sometimes think about what I'll bake the following week. Of course, this often changes, but different fruit ripens at different times. That often decides what breads and muffins we'll offer."

"I suppose." He knew his response was short, but her criticism still stung some.

"You just bought the old Baumgartner place for Ben, didn't you?"

Her question was so sunny and without undertone that he found himself answering. *"Yah."*

"Old *Frau* Baumgartner felt so bad about having had any boy *Kinder*. What were there? Seven or eight girls. I suppose *Gott* blesses how He knows best."

"Eight. And I believe *Gott* does know best." Saul hid his smile, amused by Becca's statement despite his irritation with her.

"It's unusual that all of the Baumgartner daughters' husbands had farms of their own and so far away, too. They could have leased it, I suppose."

"I suppose, but they decided to sell the land and it's close to the other property I'd purchased for Ben, so it only made sense to buy it."

"And I guess you've already decided what you'll plant there next year. You've probably decided about all your other fields, too," she observed pertly.

Closing his eyes briefly at her return to this irritating topic, Saul just said, "Maybe."

Why was he helping her? She was an annoying, sassy, young *Maedel*, even though she was cute.

"I'm just saying," she continued cheerfully, "that you could look at the options of what to plant, if you thought about it later."

"If I get this done, I can know what farm equipment I may need to buy," he defended.

"You can't plan everything out," Becca objected. "Especially in farming. The job changes with the weather and you know what basic farm equipment you'll need."

"I know," he retorted, more needled by her criticism than he wanted to admit.

Why did he even care what she thought? Becca may live on a farm, have a *Daed* and *Bruders* who worked it, but that didn't mean she knew anything about farming. Even though she was nice to look at and fun to tease.

"So," Adam said several days later as he leaned back on the porch railing, "you and Saul are seeing a lot of one another. Why? *Mamm* said he actually took you for a buggy ride the other day. I thought the two of you didn't like one another."

Becca stopped the rocking chair's motion. The moment had arrived. All through this plan of threatening Saul into helping her get Thad's attention and thwarting Chloe, Becca had known Adam presented the biggest obstacle to her success.

It seemed odd to consider him a problem when Adam had been her best friend and protector for as long as she could remember.

"Well, yes," she stammered a response. "We did drive out in his buggy."

Adam smiled—a not encouraging smile—before he said, "I repeat my question. Why? As I said, you don't even like one another."

Knowing her reply was critical to convincing him, she blurted out the first thing that came to her head. "I-I've gotten to see that Saul's not who I always thought. He's a *gut*, strong *Mann*. Haven't you always said so?"

Still propped on the railing, her brother crossed one long leg over the other. "Really? How do you think so?"

Noting that his short questions were harder to answer than if he'd expanded more, Becca said, "Don't get me wrong. He's bossy and too stiff, but Saul is…steady and steadfast. He does what he says he'll do, even if he doesn't want to."

Frowning, Adam responded, "How do you know that? I've never seen Saul do something he doesn't want to do? He's a hard *Mann* to push around."

Becca stared at her brother for a moment. She was first struck by the accuracy of his reading of Saul's character and then her thoughts bumped into her having forced Saul to play a role he didn't want to play.

Something here didn't make sense.

CHAPTER SIX

With the blue sky overhead contradicting the cool autumn breeze, Becca and Naomi unpinned the now-dried sheets from the clothesline and folded them to fit into their laundry baskets. Her skirts shifted in the air movement, Becca bent to attend to the simple task. Just then, she heard the steady clip clop of buggy horse feet coming down the drive.

Shading her eyes from sun, which seemed to stream rays into her eyes as the day closed, she turned to see who was coming.

Squinting, Becca tried to make out the identity of their caller—and felt herself stiffen. Chloe Nissly, wearing a triumphant, smug expression. With Thad driving the buggy.

Thad driving Chloe to Becca's *Haus*.

For a moment, she wished Saul were here to see the *Maedel's* satisfied expression. Then he'd understand.

"*Hallo*!!" Chloe trilled as Thad's buggy came to a stop.

Years of training in polite behavior had Becca form her expression into something like civility as she and Naomi stood beside the drive, holding full laundry baskets.

"*Hallo*." She knew she needed to say something more, but her tongue was tangled in keeping back the words she shouldn't say.

Beside her, shy Naomi stood watching.

"We just drove over for a visit," Chloe smirked. "Thad and I."

As if she couldn't see the *Mann* driving the buggy.

"Thad and I were out for a drive," Chloe expanded, "and thought we'd drop by to see you."

She simpered up at him. "Isn't Thad wonderful to take me for a drive?"

"*Yah*, of course," Thad said. "Of course, I took you out. When you told me at our last Sing that you rarely got to take buggy drives to see the countryside."

Becca almost laughed at the flash of annoyance she caught on Chloe's face at his comment.

Wishing Saul could see Chloe's display, in this moment, Becca reflected that this was the very reason she'd enlisted his help. Besting Chloe might involve rescuing Thad from her, but it was really about not letting the girl win all the time. She'd won too often and Becca told herself, in a saintly moment, that she was really doing Chloe a favor. Losing occasionally would help her soul.

Giving Thad a warm smile, Becca said, "I'm so glad you drove this way—and it was kind of you to take Chloe for a drive. Come inside. I just made some cookies and a sugar cream pie."

"That sounds wonderful," Thad said eagerly, securing the buggy reins. "A snack sounds very *gut* about now."

He got down and went to help Chloe out of the buggy.

Becca's mouth twitched as she recognized that, while the other girl was reluctant to have Becca's treats with Thad, she couldn't say this, particularly in the face of Thad's enthusiasm.

"I'll call Ezra to bring water for your horse," Naomi said, her shy gaze lowered.

Leaving her sister to stash the laundry, Becca led their guests inside. They frequently entertained friends in their home and she told herself that this was no different.

"*Hallo*, Chloe," her *Mamm* said when she took the two inside. "And Thad! How nice to see you both."

"We were just out for a drive," Chloe said, looking a little self-conscious.

"Chloe insisted we stop by," Thad said, shaking Becca's mother's hand.

"Of course," Beth Zook nodded. "We've all been doing our household tasks and taking a break is nice."

Knowing her *Mamm* would notice any coolness on her part, Becca made sure to take treats to both their visitors and to talk as easily as she could. "Are you sure you don't want another cookie?"

"*Neh, denki*," Chloe responded, her smugness muted now as if she, too, wanted to be on her best behavior with Becca's mother.

Fortunately, Thad seemed completely unaware of any undercurrents between the two girls.

Of course, Becca reflected, he pretty much seemed unaware of this, overall. She supposed that was a good thing, but it did fall in line with Saul's mild contempt of Thad.

Several mornings later, Saul sat at *Mamm's* kitchen table, enjoying the cooler early breeze that snuck through the screen door.

Glimmers of light rimmed the roof of the tall barn behind the *Haus* and the fresh air held a promise of autumn. This hour of the morning was always quiet and peaceful. He loved it.

Saul had already been out to the big structure do his early chores, only coming in to get fueled for the day. Gabe had been feeding the chickens while Ben milked the cows.

His *Mamm* stood at the stove, preparing their morning oatmeal as always and the other brothers clattered in after a while. All three *Bruders* gobbled the hot cereal. Afterwards, Gabe and Ben headed out to get the corn harvester hooked up to the farm horses in the corral.

"Before you go, Saul," his mother said when he started to leave.

He paused at the door, with an inquiring look at her as he adjusted his broad-brimmed hat on his head. "What is it, *Mamm*?"

"Saul," Susanna Stutzman paused. "If your *Daed* were here this would be a subject for you and him."

Shifting the suspenders that looped over his shoulders, he frowned, responding, "*Mamm*, you know you can say anything to me."

"*Yah*, Saul." With a decided exhalation, his mother announced in a rush, "I think it's time for you to marry. You joined the church years back and, I know, you've been busy with this farm and—and me and your *Geschwischder*."

His mouth turning down, Saul said, "*Mamm*, you know your well-being is most important to me. All of you."

"Yes, but you need more. You deserve more." She moved to lay her hand on his arm. "I know we are important to you, *der suh*, but you need a help mate, a *Frau* to work beside you."

Saul said nothing. It was almost as if she knew he were playing the courting role with Becca. That he found Becca attractive and...fun.

If it weren't so important, in their belief, not to gossip or talk about one's neighbors, he'd have wondered who had tattled about this to her. Would his *Mamm* approve of his courting Becca? The thought flashed through his head.

"We in the *familye* have occupied enough of your time, Saul. *Gott* did not wish for *Mann* to live and toil alone."

"Do you have a *Maedel* in mind?" he asked mechanically.

"This is not mine to choose," she scolded. "You must marry whomever you think is best. Of course, I don't have a girl in mind."

Susanna made clucking sounds of disapproval and Saul found himself grinning at her. "You are funny, *Mamm*."

"I am not the funny one," she said over her shoulder as she went back to the stove. "This is your choice. I'm just saying you need to attend to it."

"I will," he said, thinking of Becca as he turned to open the screen door.

"*Gut*," she said decidedly, "because you're getting too sure of yourself. Always in charge of everything! You need a *Frau* who can take you down a peg or two."

That definitely sounded like Becca, Saul thought to himself. She even challenged his farming. This thing with Becca had developed in ways he didn't expect. The image of her animated face sprang into his mind and Saul stood contemplating his unexpected reaction to her.

His mother turned back from the stove as he stood silent. "I hope I don't seem unfeeling in this, *der suh*. I only want the best for you."

He walked over and hugged her. "I know that, *Mamm*. I know."

As Saul walked out to the barn to start his day, he mulled over her words.

The trouble was that he didn't know any *Maedel* that attracted him…other than Becca, who generally annoyed him and irritated him…and made him want to kiss her.

He had to get hold of himself.

After the sermons were over the next Sunday, Becca and her sisters, Abigail and Dinah, went to help in the kitchen. The work of serving lunch to all there was big.

"You serve up the cakes and cookies," Abby directed, "and I'll serve out the meat and potatoes. Eve, I think I heard *Frau* Bassler saying there was no one pouring out lemonade."

"Of course," Dinah scurried over to take the large pitchers from the cupboards.

Becca moved to the table where the desserts had placed. The kitchen was abuzz with the voices of different women helping to get the meal out.

Slicing the different cakes, after serving up dumplings and apple fritter breads, date puddings and shoofly pie, she moved on to cut servings of the fruit pies.

In the midst of this task, Becca wondered if Thad and his family would enjoy a sweet cherry pie. She hadn't made this in a while, but whipping it up would take no time.

Several clusters of folk had stood chatting in the *Haus* as the women were busy in the kitchen and a deep, rusty voice from behind Becca asked, "How many of these did you make yourself?"

Startled, she whipped around to see Saul gazing over her shoulder at the desserts.

"A few." She looked up at him. "I hadn't realized you were here."

"*Yah*," he said, sneaking a cookie off a plate, "I was sitting behind *Frau* Beechy."

As big and stocky as was Saul, Becca nodded, knowing *Frau* Beechy was even larger. "Oh, that's why I didn't see you."

Saul grinned. "Did you miss me? You missed me, didn't you?"

Turning back to arranging the desserts, she snapped, "Of course, not."

In his annoying, lazy tone, he asked, "Aren't we supposed to eat together? To show that we're courting? Thad's here, and Chloe. You'll want them to see us together."

Becca didn't answer immediately, realizing she did want to eat with Saul, but she didn't feel particularly inclined to making sure Chloe saw them. It sounded tiring and more effort than she wanted to put out.

Leaning against the table where she was now arranging the plates of goodies, he gave her another wicked grin.

For the flash of a second, she registered that she'd never before seen this teasing, intimate side of the *Mann*.

"I guess we could get plates and eat over there under that big tree."

Just then, Abby came to ask, "Did you finish getting the desserts ready?"

"*Yah*. Everything is just about ready here," Becca responded to her elder sister, stupidly aware of Saul, loitering several feet away.

"*Gut.* The meats and vegetables should be out soon and the Drissell girls are preparing to serve the bread. We don't want you holding things up with the desserts."

Abby twitched the tablecloth to make it hang more evenly.

"No," Becca responded mechanically. "I'll have it all done in a few minutes."

"*Gut,*" Abby said again, glancing up at Saul before hurrying away.

Becca went back to slicing the last of the loaves of sweet breads.

"Quite the boss, isn't she?" Saul commented, looking after Abby as her elder sister headed back to the kitchen.

Bristling at hearing Abby described this way, Becca retorted, "Someone has to get lunch together."

Stealing another cookie—that happened to be one of hers—Saul raised his eyebrows, commenting, "You bake for paying *Englishers*. I think you can arrange a few plates of goodies. I'd think Abigail would know that you can handle this."

"Abby's just trying to keep us all organized," she defended. "She's very good at that. You should know that. Abby used to run an entire farm."

Saul's laugh was short. "*Neh.* Her husband did that. She might have run their *Haus,* but he worked the fields."

"Abby sometimes worked the fields with him," Becca insisted. "Because they hadn't yet any *Bopplin,* she sometimes worked beside Gabe."

"And now that Gabe's no longer with us, Abby gets to boss you around? Does she direct the other woman making lunch today? Some of these women were managing big households when Abby was a *Boppli* herself."

"Maybe. I never said she bossed them around." Becca felt herself getting heated in the argument.

"So, she just bosses you?" He lifted his eyebrows again, Saul's brown gazed mocking.

"*Neh*! You just don't understand," she snapped. Eating with him didn't sound so appealing now!

He continued in an even tone while dusting cookie crumbs from his hands, "I don't see that Abigail is somehow better or smarter than you. Particularly when it comes to baked goods."

"She just is," Becca said in what she hoped was a crushing reply.

Saul shrugged. "Seems like you're not giving yourself enough credit. Abigail's just a person, like us all. All striving to reflect *Gott* as best we can."

"No, she's not!" Becca returned heatedly. "She's as good as me at baking and she sews neater stitches than mine and she's really good at organizing!"

He looked at her a moment without responding, his eyes squinting a little as he stared. "You think she's better than you."

"She is! Abby does everything well!" Becca's bosom heaved as she drew angry breaths. "You know! You've been Adam's friend all these years. You've seen how she cooks and cleans! She only lives with us because Gabe died! I mean, she may not bake bread quite as good as I do, but she's great!"

"I'm not saying anything bad about Abigail, just that she's no better than you, but you clearly think she is."

"Abby's reverent and skilled and good at everything." Becca felt deflated by his level response.

Saul glanced over his shoulder at their neighbors, lining up for lunch. "You need to give yourself some credit, Becca. Stop comparing yourself to your sister and to Chloe. You're just as good."

With these words, he walked away and she stared after him, tears prickling at the back of her eyes. She felt all jumbled up and wobbly inside. His words touched her in a tender spot she hadn't even really known was there.

Not that she believed what he'd said about her and Abby, but it was still nice that he'd said it.

Becca was starting to regret making this cherry pie, she thought several days later. She'd forgotten that pitting cherries was such a messy job.

Her *Englischer* co-worker, Jennifer, stopped at the kitchen counter, on her way through the room after changing the linen in the guest rooms.

"This looks like a crime scene," she remarked, examining the counter. "What are you making?"

The counter in front of Becca did look all red and bloody.

"Cherry pie," Becca responded without enthusiasm. "It's a big mess."

Jennifer hoisted her bundled armful of soiled linens more securely. "I'm sure it'll be wonderful. How many pies are you making?"

Becca said glumly, "Five. There are more cherries to pit."

She gestured with one red hand toward a big bowlful of the fruit.

"Better you than me." The girl grinned before continuing on toward the laundry room.

Looking down at her red, stained apron, Becca mused that doing laundry sounded better right now.

She slogged on, working her way through the baskets of dark red fruit as the afternoon moved forward. Her apron only grew more stained with red splotches down the front and she could feel stickiness on her cheek. Heaven knew how it had gotten there, but Becca wasn't surprised as her hands were covered with sticky, red juice. There was even cherry juice on her long skirts, below her apron.

Becca frowned. Given that she was elbow-deep in dark, red cherry juice and had gotten stains on her sleeves, she wouldn't have been surprised if she'd gotten some of the pink/red juice on her *Kapp*. She'd probably touched it at some time.

Although she'd, of course, made pies from fresh cherries before, she'd never made quite so many. She felt honor bound to make pies for the B & B guests as she was using the kitchen and her time at work to make a pie for the Oberholtzers.

Several pie shells sat waiting to be filled, a large bowl filled with pitted and chopped cherries sat to the side. Becca sighed, her gaze falling on the basket of washed cherries still to be pitted.

This was probably a bad idea. Maybe she should save some cherries to make pies or a cobbler the next day. Thank *Gott*, the B & B was now empty, the half-dozen or so guests having gone out now to explore the town and her boss away for several more hours.

It was just as the thought slipped through her mind that Becca heard the B & B front door open. Since the large living area flowed into the open kitchen that faced the front foyer, dark cabinets lining several kitchen walls, it only took a glance over her shoulder to see Saul standing there, a big, annoying grin on his face.

"*Maedel*, what are you doing? Tell me you haven't cut yourself and are now covered in your own blood."

"I'm fine," she said, mortified at being found this way. She knew she was a stained mess.

Saul laughed. "You don't look fine. I've come to say that Adam is caught up, working in the big field."

"But, he was to pick me up after work!"

Making a gesture toward his wide chest, Saul replied, "I was asked to do that. That's why I'm here. That and because I offered to pick you up. Do you plan to drive home that way or will this red stuff wash off? Those who see us will think I'm taking you to a hospital."

Becca moved over to the large sink on the wall of cabinets to the side. She turned on the water, saying with annoyance. "Of course, it washes off. It's just cherry juice."

She thrust her hands under the water streaming faucet, frustrated that, even though the stickiness washed off, her hands were still pink.

At that very moment, she froze, hearing a very familiar—and annoying—voice call out as the noise of the front door opening registered, "*Hallo*! Becca! Thad and I have come to visit!"

"Oh, no!" she whispered in a stricken voice, casting Saul a desperate look.

While she stood frozen, her pink hands outstretched in front of her, she saw him look quickly around before he reached out to grab her arm.

Saul dragged her to the pantry and thrust her into it. Startled, Becca let out a yelp.

Following behind to draw the door closed behind them, his big hand over Becca's mouth, as if to quiet her squeak.

Surprised by his shoving her into the small space, Becca stood with him in the dark pantry, shelves laden with food stock all around them, Saul's hand still over her mouth.

She held her out her pink hands, not sure what to do with them, telling herself not to clutch Saul.

Outside of the pantry, she heard Chloe's trilling voice calling her name before the girl said something to Thad. His quiet voice could be heard responding, but all Becca registered was the darkness around her, the thundering of her own heart and the...heat of the *Mann* pressing against her in the small space.

As her eyes adjusted to the dimness, she drew in a breath heavy with the scent of Saul. He stood in front her, his hand pressed to her mouth and she suddenly swallowed hard.

She could almost feel the watchful tension in his big body and her own heartbeat began thundering against her breastbone.

All of the sudden, Becca's breath came slower, even though her heart thudded in her chest. She almost felt she was running a race. All she knew was that she hadn't ever been this near him. Sure, she'd ridden in his buggy and sat next to him at Sings, but...this felt different. Very different.

Becca forced herself to think about their situation. Anything but staring through the shadows at the firm shape of his mouth...

In the kitchen, outside the pantry doors, she heard Thad say to Chloe, "Well, she's not here. I'm not sure why you wanted to stop. Becca's obviously gone home for the day."

Chloe could be heard responding, "I just thought we could stop in and visit her."

Becca rolled her eyes in the dark pantry, thinking it might be good that Saul's hand was still over her mouth.

The girl had never stopped by the B & B before, but now that she was out with Thad, she'd wanted to stop?

It seemed unlikely to have been so simple, but Becca couldn't, at that moment, care much. Not with Saul's warm hand still pressed to her mouth.

The voices in the kitchen began to recede and still she and Saul huddled there. Becca knew they needed to make sure the pair had left before they left the closet, but all she could think about was Saul. The scent of him, the heat of his body.

She closed her eyes, trying to marshal some reason.

"I think they're probably gone now," Saul whispered, his warm breath brushing against her cheek. He lowered his hand from her mouth.

Still trying to gather her thoughts, she took a moment before nodding, whispering, "Probably."

In that frozen moment, however, neither moved. Time ticked by slowly, as if stretched out. Their gazes tangled and, before Becca knew he'd moved, Saul lowered his head and kissed her.

Becca fell into his embrace, kissing him back eagerly, reveling thoughtlessly in the heat that flashed between them. Clutching now his broad shoulders.

For such a rough and tough *Mann*, his lips felt smooth against hers and he tasted good, like nothing she'd tasted before.

Becca had been kissed before, but never like this and she'd never been kissed so thoroughly. After a moment, Saul straightened, pulling back from her. At least, as far as the small pantry would allow.

Staring up at him in the darkness, still caught up in the fire between them, her breath came shallow and fast.

"I'm sorry," he said, pushing open the pantry door. "Are you ready to go home?"

CHAPTER SEVEN

Drifting in a pond the next day, Becca brooded that she didn't know what was more annoying, Saul's insulting apology or his matter-of-fact avoidance of talking about it all the way home in the buggy. You'd almost think that kiss hadn't happened!

The kiss, though…. She warmed as she thought of it.

"You seem lost in thought," Abby commented, floating nearby.

She and her two older sisters had a few minutes between morning chores and making lunch. Abby and Dinah had agreed to come swim here with Becca since the early-August day had turned out so hot.

She stepped onto a rock that protruded from the pond, pausing to sun a little. Even now, though, with summer holding the heat of the day, the water was cool in the shade.

"Look at this!" Dinah called, jumping off a rock at the far end of the pool. As she disappeared beneath the surface, the splash sent water droplets across the pond.

"Be careful!" Abby called out, although Dinah could no longer hear.

Becca giggled and paddled across the other end of the pond.

Annoyingly, her thoughts returned to the moments in that pantry with Saul. It was annoying that he could kiss so well…and was so irritating. Maybe, he'd be okay with just kissing once in a while, she mused with an inner smile, realizing how silly that sounded, given the situation.

She wasn't sure she should share any of this with Abby and Dinah, truthfully. Well, maybe Dinah by herself, but not Abby. Her eldest *Schweschder* was such a stickler for the complete, full, absolute, total truth. Becca didn't think perfect Abby would understand her need to rescue Thad from Chloe's clutches or her agreement with Saul.

Saul...

Becca fell into remembering those breathless moments, shut in the pantry, locked in Saul's arms... His strong arms... His broad chest.

Finding herself starting to pant, she raked a hand through her wet hair and cleared her throat before dropping from the rock to swim toward her sisters.

Still, Becca felt impelled to speak about the scene in that kitchen, her all covered with cherry juice.

He'd rescued her. Saved her from being thrust into an awkward, humiliating scene with Chloe and Thad...

"Saul came to pick me up from the B & B yesterday," she blurted out.

"He did? I thought Adam was bringing you home?" Treading water nearby, Dinah frowned.

"No," Becca responded. "Saul said Adam was busy harvesting in the big field."

"Oh, yes," Abby responded, in the middle of wringing out her long hair.

Dinah swam up to a rock, tilting her head back to look up the lacy tree branches above them. "*Yah*, Adam did say he did that yesterday."

"I was making cherry pies," Becca mentioned, trying to sound casual. Not that this truthfully had to do with the cherries. "I was making them at the B & B. You know how messy cherries can be."

Abby nodded. "They certainly can be and you did come home looking a real mess. I noticed."

Dinah giggled. "Cherries are a mess, but they taste so good!"

"Of course, you noticed!" Becca retorted. "I was covered with cherry juice when Saul came to pick me up. I mean, covered!

Splotched all over in red juice! I guess I looked like I'd rolled in cherries. I did wash my hands, but afterwards they were all pink!"

Her older sister chuckled. "You did look bad."

"Guess who stopped by the B & B just when I was such a mess? There I was, up to my elbows in cherries, covered with juice. Cherries everywhere. I didn't even finish, though. The pies are still there. I just stuck them and the extra cherries into the B & B's refrigerator."

"Someone you know stopped by?" Dinah asked. "I assume the B & B guests come in and out."

"Why didn't you finish them? Who stopped by?" Abby climbed out of the water to sit at the edge of the pond.

"I—I got interrupted."

Her sisters waited for her to go on, Dinah pausing closed to Becca.

"Chloe stopped at the B & B just then!" Becca said. "And she just happened to have Thad Oberholtzer with her."

Dinah looked appalled, apparently getting the situation. "Oh! No!"

"You certainly weren't in any shape to have visitors," Abby observed. "Chloe Nissley? That girl from your class in school?"

"*Yah*." Becca pulled another face. "She came by with no notice. Just stopping in when I looked my worst. Right when Saul had come to pick me up for Adam."

"Sounds like Chloe Nissly," Dinah observed. "She always has the knack of catching me at my worst."

Abby started to laugh.

"Go ahead and laugh," Becca said, not feeling the urge to join in her sister's amusement. "It wasn't funny to me!"

"No," Abigail said, still smiling. "I don't suppose it was. What did you do? Did they see you like that?"

"Yes, did she see you?" Dinah exclaimed.

"*Neh*, thank goodness, Saul had come to pick me up for Adam—like I said—and, when Chloe showed up like that, he shoved me in the pantry, so she and Thad didn't see me in all my messy state. I'm glad he thought fast," she said, not mentioning that Saul had joined her there.

Becca was still sorting that through and she just didn't want to talk about it yet. "He kind of saved me."

Her mind was flooded again with that moment. How hot the pantry seemed, all of a sudden. How Saul had filled up the space.

She drew a deep breath.

"My apron and my dress were cherry-stained by that time," Becca went on. "I'd even gotten cherry juice on my face!" She paddled next to Abby, her story falling from her mouth as she slipped through the cool pond water.

"Do you know I found red spots on my *Kapp* when I changed?"

Laughing, Dinah paddled nearby. "You were a mess!"

"*Yah*, I saw that. I've never seen cherry pie making go so bad," Abby said. "You are such a messy baker!"

Becca made a face. "Not usually this messy."

"This is true." Dinah agreed.

Abby floated nearby. "I thought you liked Chloe. Isn't she your friend?"

"We went to school together, but I wouldn't call Chloe a friend."

"*Gott* has directed us to be loving toward all," Abby reminded her, clearly hearing Becca's lack of enthusiasm. "Are you being fair to this girl?"

"I can see why she wouldn't be." Dinah muttered. "Not with Chloe Nissly."

Even with her sister's words, Becca blurted out, "Chloe's not kind or fair. Why do you think she had Thad Oberholtzer drive her to where I work? She was showing off! I don't think the *Ordnung* recommends that!"

"That sounds just like something she'd do!"

"It also doesn't recommend that we look at the speck in our neighbor's eye, ignoring the chunk of wood in our own," was Abby's calm response.

Becca knew she should be chastised by this, but her indignation with Chloe was strong!

"You are such a prude sometimes." Swimming to the other side of the pond, Dinah threw her response to Abby's words over her shoulder.

"You wouldn't talk about the 'speck' in her eye if you'd seen her with Thad," Becca returned with spirit.

Abby had been chastising Becca her whole life and, as the younger sister, Becca was used to it by now. Besides, no one could be as good as her faultless sister. Even Dinah acknowledged this. Becca had given up trying.

"Mmmm," was Abby's only reply.

Silence fell between them as the three sisters floated in the shadowed pond.

Having no distraction, the remembrance of Saul's strong embrace crept back into Becca's consciousness and she let herself dwell for a moment on the wonderful, strange sensation that had sprung up in her at his kiss.

She wanted more kisses from Saul…and this, in itself, was weird. Saul!

It was irritating that he'd said nothing as he drove her home, but she didn't really know what to say herself. Maybe not speaking about it was the way to go.

He'd saved her in that moment, but it was starting to look like he regretted the whole thing.

"No, no." Becca chuckled several days later when Saul tried to flatten the biscuit dough laying on the counter in front of them.

"I don't even know why I'm doing this," he commented. It did no good to tell himself that he'd come here to visit his good friend, Adam. It would have made more sense to stay far from this house and this silly *Maedel*.

It wasn't time for him to pick a wife and, even if there weren't other things that needed tending to, Becca wasn't the woman for him. Besides, Becca had threatened to expose him. She was blackmailing him into this courting farce because she wanted Thad. Not him.

"You wanted to make biscuits!" She laughed again, taking the floury rolling pin. "You're not so much doing this as trying to do it."

"See? You're a better baker. Let's each do what we know." He needed to leave the kitchen.

Saul didn't know why he'd succumbed to the silly impulse to kiss her when they'd hidden in the B & B's pantry. Some sort of craziness must have pushed him into it. The same sort of nuttiness that had led him to find an excuse to come here today, he told himself harshly.

She passed the rolling pin over the dough in a practiced sweep. "Don't be so hasty to give up. Here."

Despite the prompting in his brain, Saul took the pin she held out.

"Try it again. Just don't press down as much."

"*Maedel*, when will I ever need to do this?" Saul cocked an eyebrow at her. She'd hauled him into her craziness and Saul didn't know why. He also didn't know why he'd agreed. Becca couldn't do anything to him. He'd already made his peace about the *Englischer* incident and he'd spoken to his bishop.

"You never know, you might need this knowledge someday. What if you were snowed in with only *Menner*? You'd be the only one to know this and the others would be very grateful to have biscuits."

"Very, very unlikely." He rolled the pin over the dough again.

"*Yah*. That's better. Even a little less pressure." She leaned close to pick up the dough again, her practiced hands quickly balling it up.

Finding himself inhaling the fresh scent of her as she brushed his shoulder, Saul briefly closed his eyes, trying to remember that this was Adam's little sister and she'd been a pain all their growing-up years.

Becca's *Grossmammie* Ruth came into the kitchen then. Seeing the two of them standing beside the floured countertop, the old woman smiled pleasantly, saying, "Are you giving baking lessons, Becca? You could have started with sugar cookies or oatmeal molasses crisps. *Menner* generally have a sweet tooth."

"Actually," Saul mused, "those sound good. Let's wait until you're baking cookies. I don't think I'm any good at making biscuits."

The girl beside him gave him a chiding, teasing smile. "You just want another baking lesson."

Amidst the chuckles from Becca and her *Grossmammie's* laughter, Saul gave himself grief for wanting exactly that.

"Well," he said, dusting the flour from his hands, "I should probably get back to my farm. Tell Adam I came by to see him."

Without waiting for either woman to reply, he grabbed his broad hat from a peg near the kitchen door and said, *"Goedemorgen."*

Becca watched him go, from where she stood behind the counter, the flattened biscuit dough before her.

"Well, that was sudden," her *Grossmammie* said. "Is he usually so abrupt?"

Not sure what to say in response, Becca picked up the rolling pin, coasting it again over the dough. "He can be, sometimes, I suppose."

Grossmammie Ruth chuckled richly. "Not the sort of *Buwe* I'd think you want to spend time with. Although Saul can be charming, when he laughs. It's so unexpected, then boom. He laughs with his whole self."

"*Yah*, that's true," Becca said slowly. And he had stood here and let her lecture him about making biscuits.

She found herself laughing, remembering it.

"We'll see him again, as he's Adam's particular friend." Her *Grossmammie* threaded a kitchen towel into the rack and then went to ease herself into the rocking chair that sat by the fireplace the kitchen shared with their living room.

"*Yah*, we will," Becca murmured. That moment in the B & B pantry with him flashed through her mind then, the silence between them. The press of Saul's lips to hers. The warm scent of him.

Mentally shaking free of that captivating memory, she said, "He's certainly not always abrupt."

She'd never expected to see him here this morning or thought that he'd make biscuits with her. This time with him was as unexpected as his saving her when Chloe had traipsed in with Thad.

"I guess-I guess Saul can sometimes even be helpful. He acted fast when I was a mess at the B & B."

Her grandmother looked an inquiry at these words.

"I was baking cherry pies. You know what a mess cherries can make."

Her *Grossmammie* nodded. "Yes, *Gott's* stain. Cherry juice. Yummy fruit, though."

"When Chloe Nissley showed up with a *Mann* and I was a mess!" Becca started cutting out the biscuits, using the rim of a water glass. "I was in shock—Chloe had never come to the B & B before—and Saul acted fast, pulling me into the B & B pantry, where I couldn't be seen."

Grossmammie Ruth nodded, her mouth stretched into a musing expression. "There's a lot to be said for a *Mann* who helps one out of a difficult situation."

A week later, Becca thrust her needle through the fabric in the quilt frame in front of her and pricked the finger waiting under the quilt. With the damaged finger in her mouth, she sent a weak half-smile to Chloe, wondering why she'd thought coming to her rival's *Haus* was a good idea.

She just hated to back down from a challenge…and that was what Chloe's invitation seemed.

"I'm so glad you could come visit with us," Chloe said with what looked to Becca like an insincere smile.

Pulling her finger from her mouth, she said with just as much honesty, "*Denki.*"

Chloe's two eldest sisters sat on the other side of the frame, diligently stitching and sending Becca smiles whenever they looked up. She'd bet they had heard an earful about her from their *Schweschder*. Becca had known Damaris and Miriam all her life, just as she'd known Chloe forever, but she'd always gotten along with Chloe's sisters.

"Isn't it hot this year?" Damaris asked.

Knowing heat was difficult during pregnancy, Becca said, "*Yah.* Thankfully, it only lasts a short time each August."

Damaris had married a year before and Becca reckoned by her belly size that she was likely in the early stages of bearing her first child. Talking about pregnancy was considered a form of bragging and the *Amisch* never did this.

Miriam was single still and looked to remain that way for a while, since she was shy and rarely spoke unless spoken to. She was a year older than Becca and Chloe and even though she went to Sings, she didn't often talk to the *Menner* there. Becca couldn't ever remember her driving home with a *Buwe*.

Becca herself had driven home with a number of *Menner*, but at that moment, she only thought of Saul…

Falling into abstraction, she again remembered his calloused fingers against her lips, holding her silent in the darkened pantry.

Becca took a deep breath and jerked herself back to the present. It was foolish to let this moment replay in her mind.

As the sisters talked of garden crops to be harvested soon and those to be planted in the next year, her sight blurred as she stared down at the quilt on which they worked. In those moments, she didn't reproach herself that her stitches weren't as small and neat as Abby's. Instead, she let herself remember being pulled close and held against Saul's broad chest in that pantry.

Maybe she needed to kiss Thad, she mused. Saul's kiss surely couldn't have been as earth-shattering as she remembered. It had just surprised her.

Blinking, she again focused on her stitches. *Yah*, she'd found her gaze tangled in his when they were in that darkened pantry. On some level, she'd recognized an impossible possibility—a breathless connection with a *Mann* she'd never even liked.

"...when Thad and I were out driving in his buggy," Chloe's voice intruded, "we stopped by the B & B to see you Becca, but someone else must have been baking there. You weren't anywhere around, but there was a mess on the counter."

Becca took a second to thrust her needle into the quilt. She pasted a bright smile on her face. "*Yah*, others who work there do bake some."

"Well, it was quite a mess," her bogus friend said. "I hope whoever it was cleaned up after themselves."

"They did." Becca felt bad about being deceitful, but it seemed she was too far into this to do otherwise, at this point.

"You're driving out with Thad a lot," Damaris observed, her mouth lifting in a small smile.

Chloe simpered in response, ducking her head bashfully. "Thad's been very attentive. He's shy, though. I know he wants to drive me out in his buggy, but he sometimes hesitates to ask. I think he just struggles to do this, thinking he's asking too often."

Sure, thought Becca, mentally rolling her eyes again. That was the case. Thad wanted to ask Chloe, but didn't know how or thought he shouldn't ask so often.

"Some *Menner* need a nudge," Damaris agreed, casting Miriam a sideways glance. "*Maedels* just have to know when to do this."

"I see," Chloe said with a smirk, "that you've driven home from Sings with Saul Stutzman and you've eaten with him after services several times."

"*Yah*." Becca was feeling a little defiant by now."

"Isn't he, well, older and very serious?" Chloe asked, still with that irritating smile on her face.

Becca knew the goal of this whole thing was to convince Chloe—and Thad—that she had another suitor, but the words that came out of her mouth were surprisingly honest.

"Saul's not serious all the time." She studied the quilt for a moment before going on. "He's actually…funny sometimes…and nice."

She looked up. "He's not anything like he seems, at first."

As the words came out of her mouth, Becca realized that this was true. Before, she'd only known him as a pest that hung out with her *Bruder*, Adam. In a bizarre twist, this matter of Chloe and Thad had shown her a different side of Saul.

It was a development she hadn't expected.

"I've also discovered, when driving out with him, that Thad's very attentive," Chloe said, her mouth curling in that irritating smile. "We've gone driving together several times already. We were out in his buggy when we came by the B & B to see you, Becca. Of course, I don't have to work outside our home, but I know some do."

With another wave of annoyance at this aspersion cast on her family, Becca responded with irritation. "My *Mamm* and *Daed* work hard for our *familye*. It only seems reasonable that we *Kinder* work hard, too."

Damaris said, "This is true for most all."

Miriam nodded in agreement.

"Oh! Of course," Chloe said. "I didn't mean to imply otherwise."

"And not only that," Becca added in a strong voice, "we *Kinder* have always been taught that work brings us closer to *Gott*."

"This is true," her rival said, another smirking smile on her face. "We all work, too. Just in the home here."

"We have all been taught," Becca declared in a clincher, "to work in the home and be employed elsewhere, if possible. *Gott* loves a cheerful worker."

Several nights later, the sky was dark around Saul and Adam, glimmering stars winking above them. The pair sat perched on a wood fence that formed a pen by the Zook barn.

"Supper was *gut*," Saul remarked. "Your *Mamm* and sisters feed you well."

"They do," Adam agreed, turning his head to say, "Becca made the biscuits tonight. Are her biscuits why you're driving with her more? I've noticed that the two of you are seeing more of one another. Didn't you bring her home after the last Sing?"

Having expected for some time that this conversation would take place, Saul wasn't shaken. It was probably better, he thought, that Adam had spoken to him about this, rather than Becca.

He didn't directly answer the question his friend had asked, waiting several beats before responding, "You, yourself, asked me to pick Becca up from her job at the B & B."

"I did, but this has gone beyond just picking her up, hasn't it?"

Saul laughed. "A *Mann* drives a *Maedel* out in his buggy— and picks her up for his friend—and that means something is going on between them?"

"It's not something you've done with my sister before," Adam observed. "As a matter of fact, I didn't think the two of you even liked one another."

"You'll be relieved to know that I'm discovering she's not as annoying as I thought her."

Adam chuckled. "I've always liked Becca. Of all my sisters, she's least likely to get ruffled about things. This seems like something more, though? And don't give me any silliness about you picking Becca up for me!"

Saul shrugged.

Whenever he'd come to see Adam, he'd actually always enjoyed the back-and-forth arguments between he and Becca.

Why he'd agreed to her silly farce wasn't totally clear to him. Even less clear was why he'd kissed her in that pantry. She'd been right there, wide eyed and covered in cherry juice. A total mess.

And suddenly he was kissing her.

Debiel that he was.

He really didn't care about Chloe Nissley or Thad Oberholtzer…but he suppose he'd agreed to this silly pretense because he hadn't liked the idea of Becca asking another *Mann* to do this for her. He certainly wasn't about to commit himself to Becca, at this point, or to any other *Maedel* now. He had too much on his plate, so it had made sense to let her think he was frightened of her threats to disclose his foolish, impulsive action with the *Englischer* car.

"*Menner* drive *Maedels* home from Sings all the time," was all he said after several moments.

Adam laughed. "You and Becca. This seems like a startling thing…and then not. I can see the two of you together."

"Don't get ahead of yourself, friend. I never said this was a serious thing. I just drove her home." He preferred keeping his thoughts close to himself. If he liked Becca, this wasn't a matter to be shared with anyone else, beyond this little nonsense of hers.

"Several times," Adam scoffed. "You, friend, may be deeper into this than you thought."

Saul was starting to think this might be the case.

CHAPTER EIGHT

"Thad would, too, make a good husband!" Becca disputed hotly the next Sunday, her squabble with Saul silly, as she was, even now, riding home from the sermon in his buggy.

"I don't see why you're even slightly interested in Thad Oberholtzer," Saul replied without a great deal of inflection in his voice.

"Thad is a very nice *Mann*! I don't know why I'm even arguing this with you." She tried to make her declaration sound lofty. If she could have managed this without her cheeks reddening, it might have worked. She could feel the heat in her face.

Please, Gott, she prayed, *help me not sound like a child!*

"He may be nice," Saul returned "but that doesn't mean he'd be a *gut* husband. He's too much like a little *Buwe*. You'd spend all your marriage changing his pants."

Becca gasped. "That's not true! You're a *bisskatz* to say so. That's just mean!"

From his seat beside her in the buggy, his large hands relaxed on the reins, Saul laughed and shrugged. "I'm simply saying what I see. This whole business is you trying to rescue Thad from Chloe's grips, like a farmer rescuing a chicken from a fox. That doesn't make the chicken a *gut* husband."

"Thad is not a chicken!" Beyond prayer, she drew in a deep breath to calm herself. "It's not very nice to call Chloe a fox, either."

Not that she actually disagreed with this.

Saul laughed, a gravelly sound in his throat. "You're the one trying to save little Thad from her, like grabbing him from her jaws."

"No. No," she repeated, trying to speak calmly. "As I've always said, Chloe just seems to think she can have any *Mann* and Thad deserves better."

"But Thad can't see this himself—that Chloe doesn't really care about him—so you must rescue him. Chicken and fox."

Annoyed by his conclusion, but not able to think of a good response, Becca simply shook her head. "You're basically too blind to see Thad's good qualities, that's all."

Saul turned his head to look at her. "What would you say are Thad's 'good qualities'?"

Caught up in her argument with him, Becca couldn't reply right away. "Well...he's nice! He isn't mean to anyone. He's a good *Amisch Mann* and goes to sermons every service."

She stumbled to a stop, sitting appalled at not being able to think of anything else. Thad was a nice man and, surely, there was more to him.

Surprised that Saul didn't pounce on her lame response, she sat next to him on the buggy seat, resisting the urge to close her eyes in frustration.

"Would you like to come to dinner with my *familye*?" Saul asked abruptly. "Tomorrow night, perhaps?"

"I would like that," Becca said, the words coming out of her mouth a surprise to her. When she considered a moment, as he guided the buggy toward her *Haus*, she acknowledged to herself that she meant her words. She would like to eat with Saul's family and wished, for a moment, that it wasn't just for show.

"Good," he said, clicking his tongue to encourage the buggy horse up an incline.

Saul couldn't say why he'd invited Becca to eat supper with his family. He mused on the question the next evening before deciding not to delve into it too deeply. She looked very right, sitting there next to his sister, though.

He'd been sitting right there beside her in the buggy, having that ridiculous argument with her, and the invitation came spontaneously out of his mouth.

"Here are the potatoes, Becca," Saul's *Mamm*, said, passing Becca a bowl with a smile.

"Thank you, *Frau* Stoltfus," Becca said with her dimpled grin. "Saul has said what a good cook you are."

Giving the plate of food in front of him a small smirk, Saul registered having a glow of warmth in his chest. Again, he didn't want to think about it too much. This was a pretense, his courtship of Becca. He needed to remember that.

"*Denki*," his *Mamm* responded. "I'm grateful to have Amity and Leah help a lot with the meals."

An hour later, Becca crowded in with his chattering sisters at the counter sink, washing, drying and putting away the dishes. She'd insisted on this despite Saul having intervened to say guests didn't clean up.

While the girls prattled away, he sat out on the back porch that faced the big barn. His youngest brother was perched on the porch railing opposite him while his fifteen-year-old brother sat on a porch swing they'd constructed for their *Mamm*.

"You've never had a *Maedel* over to supper," Ben commented in a sly tone.

"She seems nice," said Gabe innocently. Only two years younger than Ben, he hadn't yet entered his annoying years.

"*Yah*," Ben needled in his teasing manner, "she seems...nice."

"Perhaps you should go help Abe check on the draft horses in the barn," Saul said finally.

"I think he can manage fine," Ben returned. "He's to have his own farm, soon."

Saul made no response to this, thinking it was to be expected that seventeen-year-old Ben would have something to say.

"She seems like a very nice *Maedel*," young Gabe offered.

"She is," Saul said, rising from the bench he'd occupied.

Just then, the kitchen screened door opened and Becca came out, followed by his younger sister, Leah.

Heat crawling up his neck, he hoped Becca hadn't heard the last bit of his conversation with his *Bruders*.

Saul uncharacteristically hurried into speech. "Leah, did you get the goats in the new pen?"

His sister—already twenty-one and spending time with one particular young *Mann*—made a wry face and said, "I think those goats are of the devil, Saul. Why did you not tell me this?"

Glad to refocus his attention, he said sternly, "Leah, devilish or not, the goats need to be moved, so we can put the farm horses in that pen."

"I know," his sister responded, making a wry face, "and I tried, but they kept running around. Some even ran away! Cannot Gabe help me move them?"

"Gabe has been helping us harvest the south field. If you're to help your eventual husband run his farm, you'll need to do these things yourself," he said in a more austere tone than he'd have used if he weren't as off-balance with Becca there.

"You're right. I understand," she responded without any resentment. "I'll get them moved tomorrow."

With the scene playing out between the two *Geschwischder*, his two brothers had disappeared, heading to the barn, while his older sister, Amity, had gone back into the kitchen.

"*Goedenavond*," Leah said, leaving them to go into the kitchen herself.

Becca stood, alone now, on the porch with Saul, his head turned to watch his sister leave, indignation swelling in her breast. "Well, that was just mean!"

She'd been preparing to sit in the porch swing, but bounced up to face him.

He turned to look at her. "What? What are you saying?"

The evening light growing fainter, she stalked over to where he stood. There was a time when she'd have hesitated to say anything this critical and direct to Adam's friend, but their ruse had thrown her in Saul's company often and she didn't feel the need to tiptoe around him now.

"What you said to poor Leah! That was just mean!"

He stiffened. "Leah understands me very well. She's to marry a farmer...one day. How she handles livestock is very important."

"Maybe," Becca acknowledged, a farmer's *dochder* herself, "but you didn't have to speak to her so harshly. You could have been more kind!"

"She's my sister," Saul waved a dismissive hand. "She understands me very well. Leah's accustomed to how I speak."

"She probably is," Becca returned tartly, "but that doesn't mean your words to her were nice. You sounded angry and arrogant."

He walked over to the swing she'd abandoned, lowering himself onto it. "Don't be silly."

Becca wasn't concerned that he looked irritated and indifferent, his face assuming the mask-like expression she'd seen before. She needed Saul to hear her.

Following him to sit in a chair positioned near the swing, she sat, asking, "Did you offer methods she might use with the goats? The animals can be difficult to corral."

"Leah's handled goats before and managed just fine," he responded in an acid tone.

"I don't doubt it, but that doesn't mean you were helpful."

"She doesn't need my help!" he retorted.

"Have you thought about her asking your other sister for help? If Gabe is busy, Amity might be free."

His eyes narrowed. "Why is this even your problem?"

"Because I like Leah...and you...sort of. And I don't think you were nice to her. Doesn't *Gott* instruct us to be kind?"

Saul drew in a deep breath, clearly battling with himself before he responded. "I'm glad you like Leah."

"I, also, want her to think—" Becca ducked her head, suddenly feeling weirdly awkward. She hadn't felt self-conscious or uncomfortable before in this conversation. "I also want others to think well of you. You would be better to be less...stern. Not so rigid. You need to think of possibilities, of how things can be done other ways."

She raised her head to look at him, then, and was surprised to find a glimmer of a smile of Saul's face. Not a smirk or frown, but an actual smile.

"Perhaps you're right. You may have a point."

The smile and his words startled her and Becca let out a breath she hadn't known she was holding.

"There are always different ways to accomplish a thing, Saul. She doesn't have to wrangle the goats by herself now."

"No, but she should be able to do it herself. She will not always have Amity to help her."

"That's true," Becca agreed in fairness, "but there are still other ways to move the goats. Leah can block off parts of the pen, so they can go only out the gate she wishes."

Saul was silent.

"See?" she said. "Always other paths. You can't just look at a problem only one way. I know. I've moved goats."

"*Yah*," Saul said, again with that glimmering smile. "I can see that you have. I'd like to have seen that."

Becca made a face at him and he laughed.

"I just want you to more kind to your sister."

"I appreciate that," Saul said after a moment and they swung gently to and fro.

For several moments, silence descended between them and the sounds of the evening rose up across the yard, the shadows deepening.

She didn't know why it was so important to her that Saul not be harsh.

The sounds of the two sisters in the kitchen could be heard and once Saul's mother joined their laughter.

Finally, his deep, rusty voice broke the silence between them. "I've always regretted slashing the *Englischer's* tires."

The swing's chain creaked a little as he swung back and forth.

"Then, why did you do it? It seems…" The fact that he'd even brought up this topic startled her and Becca held her breath, waiting for him to make a dismissive comment.

"It seems unlike you to do something so…" she said after a minute. She knew some of the event from Adam's remarks, but she'd always had a hard time seeing purposeful, in control Saul doing such an impetuous thing.

He was so deliberate and grown-up. Not the sort of *Mann* to do destructive things for a lark. She could see foolish *Menner* on *rumspringa* doing this, but not Saul.

He sat swinging in silence so long that she'd begun thinking he wasn't going to answer. Finally, Saul said in his deep voice, "I would do anything for my *familye*. For my own."

Becca waited for him to go on.

"Back in those days, all my brothers and sisters were small, at least smaller."

Through the *Haus* windows, the gleam of lamp light could be seen and Becca could smell wood burning. Someone must have lit the fireplace and that, too, would be adding light to the living room.

Saul's face, however, was in shadow, the light having gone out of the sky.

"It was just chance that I'd taken Leah into the grain store with me that day."

As he talked, some parts of the story came back to her. Leah had been hurt by the *Englischer* car.

"You slashed the tires of the *Englisher* who almost hurt Leah, wasn't it?" The words sprang impulsively out of Becca.

He went on as if she hadn't spoken. "Leah and I were walking through the town. I'd just picked her up from her friend, Grace Bacher's *Haus*."

Sitting in silence, she waited for him to go on. "Leah was a girl then, only a young *Maedel*, and the town street was busy. I was aware enough to keep her on the sidewalk, away from the traffic…, but I stopped. Just the once. I was scraping something off the bottom of my shoe, when…."

Realizing she was holding her breath as he talked, Becca sucked air into, blurting out, "And the *Englischer's* car?"

"The *Mann* was driving too fast, way too fast on a road along which people walked."

Becca knew all too well the danger that fast *Englischer* cars presented to the slower buggy. Too many *Amisch* had met their ends in the crashes that sometimes resulted.

"But Leah's here. She's fine." Swallowing, Becca waited for Saul to finish.

"Only because I saw the *Englischer* car headed toward her and—and pulled her out of the way. Well, almost out of the way."

Her mouth falling open in dismay, Becca's gaze was glued to his face.

"That must have been really scary." It hadn't seemed all that real to her when Adam told her about the event, but now—listening to Saul talk about it—she was angry with the *Englisch* driver herself.

Saul looked down, drawing in a deep breath before saying, "I have thanked *Gott* many, many times that she was only grazed. That I happened to look up just then."

"Oh, you must have been so upset!"

"And angry," Saul said, his jaw clenching. "I carried her home, all battered. I didn't know where exactly she'd been hit. The *Englischer* car just raced on. I don't think the driver even knew he'd grazed Leah."

Becca's hand pressed to her chest, she tried to connect the Leah that she known all these years with the hurt child she must have been. "It was a blessing, indeed, that you happened to turn! How badly was she hurt?"

"She was greatly bruised and walked with a stick for a while, but thankfully she recovered completely. I should have been watching her better." His face frozen in self-reproach, Saul gazed angrily at the toe of his shoe.

Becca couldn't remember hearing anything about this, at the time. She tried to remember Leah being absent from school. Perhaps this had happened in the summer break.

"I walked back—after taking her home—to get the doctor to come to tend her." He lifted his head and looked at her with dark somber eyes. "And I happened to see the same *Englischer* car. It had distinctive markings and it was parked at an *Englischer* motel."

The sick feeling that had gripped Becca's stomach had her scooting forward on her seat. This was nothing she'd imagined when she forced him into taking part in her plan. Not really. Suddenly, she felt she shouldn't hold him to their agreement. Her pretense had grown and grown into something she hadn't planned.

She shouldn't have done it. She should release him from this agreement. Let him go back to doing what he wanted.

And yet...

Becca didn't want to let him go. The realization hit her in her chest.

She didn't want to just have Saul be Adam's friend and nothing special to her anymore. This had originally been about besting Chloe with Thad. Now...

Now, Thad seemed very faint in her mind and she wondered why she'd ever been shallow enough to care what Chloe thought. If Thad let himself get snared into marrying Chloe, maybe that was as it should be.

Becca wasn't even near to seeing all. That was *Gott's* work, not hers.

She swallowed hard, staring at Saul. She had no right to force him into this. She should end this now, but she didn't—she didn't want to do that. Didn't want to let him recede back into being just Adam's annoying friend.

She didn't know why, but the idea of seeing him only when he dropped by to visit Adam...was hard .

Becca swallowed again. She didn't exactly know what Saul was to her now, but he was something...and she didn't want that to change.

CHAPTER NINE

"*Grossmammie* Ruth," Becca said, the next morning as she raked up leaves that had fallen on their garden as autumn drew nearer, "how did you know you wanted to marry *Grossdaddie*?"

Sitting across the garden plot, her grandmother lifted her gray, *kapped* head to look at Becca. *Grossmammi* Ruth chuckled. "That was a long time ago, child."

"*Yah*, but I'll bet you still remember," Becca responded shrewdly.

The older woman sat on a low stool, pulling up weeds that had sprung up through the brown stems that poked through the garden beds.

Her grandmother smiled at her response. "I do."

Turning toward her, Becca leaned on the rake in her hands. "Tell me, then. How did you know?"

All since last evening on Saul's porch—his deep voice talking of the *Englischer* car having grazed poor Leah—Becca had thought about her own response to his story. It had never seemed like this when Adam first told her. She'd been wrong before, but never had she felt so wrong. She knew she should release Saul from this mockery into which she'd drawn him...but she really didn't want to do so. The thought of not taking buggy rides with him... Of Saul not sitting next to her at lunch after services....

She just didn't want to.

"Becca, dear," her *Grossmammie* said, "have you found a boy you want to marry?"

"I don't know." She looked down at the garden plot she was raking.

"What about this Saul Stutzman you've been driving out with?"

Becca felt color bloom in her cheeks. "My question was about you and *Grossdaddi*."

"I know this very well, *Maedel*."

"Why, then, are you asking me about Saul?" She loved her *Grossmammi* Ruth living with them. The old woman always had a cheerful laugh or a warm hug for her and Becca had respect for her grandmother's opinion. "What do you think of him?"

She said this very casually, but peeped a glance at her *Grossmammi* to see her reaction.

The old lady considered the matter before saying in her forthright manner, "I like Saul. I always have. He's level-headed and cares for his *familye*. He also has a good sense of humor, even though, he keeps this hidden."

She pulled a few more weeds before looking up to add, "Saul's always been a *gut* friend to Adam. By the way, have you noticed Adam driving out any particular *Maedel*?"

Becca laughed, before saying primly, "*Grossmammi*, you know that's not our business!"

"Of course, it's not. We are told to be modest and private," her grandmother responded after a few minutes, "but that doesn't mean we don't notice things."

Chuckling at this, Becca let the smile fade from her lips before asking, "How are we to choose a mate, Grandmother? I'm serious."

Her *Grossmammi* drew in and let out a long breath. "Sweet girl, this is different for different people."

Waiting for her grandmother to continue, Becca set the rake aside to go sit on the ground next to where the old woman sat.

"I married your *Grossdaddi* after he—he seemed to laugh at all my jokes. He never spoke meanly about anyone around us— even as a *Buwe*—and he…" Her grandmother seemed to fall into remembering. "Your *Grossdaddi* and I spent a lot of time together. He liked being around me and I liked being around him."

"You always liked one another?" She couldn't say that she and Saul had ever really liked one another. He'd been off with the older boys at school.

Her grandmother laughed suddenly. "Not always, Becca. We sometimes really argued and disagreed."

"After you were his *Frau*?"

"Then and before. When we were in school, and later, when we courted." Her grandmother reflected a moment. "We always worked things out in the end, though, and *Grossdaddi* helped me learn, too. I had to slow down—particularly as we aged. It is natural to slow down, then, but I had to learn to do it."

"You always seem so *schmaert*, *Grossmammi*. It's hard to think of you needing to learn anything. Of course, *Grossdaddi* was wonderful, too." Becca pulled at some weeds in front of her.

"*Yah*, he was wonderful," her grandmother gave a little hiccuping laugh, "but I needed to learn many things. I think we all need to learn things all through life."

Grossmammi Ruth was silent for a moment. "Probably the hardest thing was learning how to live my life without him."

Becca looked at her grandmother, retaining a respectful silence.

After a moment, *Grossmammi* Ruth shook off her melancholia to smile at Becca. "Marry someone who's good for you, granddaughter. Someone you like and who likes you."

She just looked at her grandmother, her confused questions still hovering in her head.

"There are *Menner* who will do well enough. Those who make a good living and are pleasant enough, but this kind didn't occupy my mind, didn't snare my attention like *Grossdaddi*. We argued and disagreed, but…I just knew I was better with him than without him."

"You were better with him than without him," Becca repeated slowly, her vague suspicion shifting into a glaring realization. It was Saul.

Saul who annoyed her...but made her better. Beside him, Thad was a pale shadow, one of those "pleasant enough *Menner*" her grandmother had described.

She could hear her heartbeat in her ears. She'd never have believed this—she had feelings for Saul Stutzman. Saul.

Saul who annoyed her and who'd teased her for years. Saul, who she'd blackmailed into acting like he liked her.

Becca felt sick to her stomach. She stopped plucking at the weeds in the garden dirt and just sat there, grief and regret and dismay welling in her.

If this was what it felt like to realize she loved a *Mann*, she couldn't see why girls longed for it.

She couldn't deny it, though. She loved Saul.

"Dinah," Becca rolled out a pie crust later that day. "Have you ever done something you really shouldn't have?"

"Of course," her older sister said, making a rueful, laughing face. "I think everyone has."

"Not Abby," Becca said glumly.

"No," Dinah lifted her eyebrows. "Probably not."

Becca's gaze blurred as she looked at the crust in front of her. She'd messed up so badly. How could Saul ever forgive her? She know *Gott* forgave mistakes. That didn't mean she could forgive herself, which made no sense, but so it was. If she couldn't forgive herself, she knew Saul couldn't.

"I have to admit," Adam said a day later as he tossed hay into the buggy horse's hay rack, "For a time, I thought this whole thing between you and Saul was a prank."

102

Becca took a deep breath, bracing herself against the wall of the stall, before asking, "What do you mean?"

She hated lying to her brother, but she didn't know how to tell him the truth. She wasn't sure what Saul felt for her, if anything, and now she loved him.

It was all a mess.

"Well, it just wasn't obvious," Adam said. "I mean, you always hated each other."

With a sinking heart, she questioned, "You thought, Saul hated me?"

It was such a harsh word.

Her brother shrugged. "Not any more than you disliked him, but I was clearly wrong. At first, I thought the two of you were joking everyone."

She looked down. Telling Adam that she'd coerced Saul into helping her beat out Chloe wasn't an option and, now that she'd fallen in love with Saul, it didn't even tell the whole story.

Not that the whole story was even worth telling. Saul had kissed her that once, but that didn't really change anything.

Becca swallowed hard. She'd like to kiss Saul again.

"It's a little *narrish*," Adam said, in an offhand voice. "Seeing the two of you together. "Right, somehow, but weird."

She sat silent, not knowing how to respond. She knew there was little hope of a happy outcome to this mess.

"Just the thought of the two of you marrying is a little startling. Of course, each have to decide their own best path."

"I love him," Becca blurted out. "I didn't mean to fall in love with Saul, but I did."

Hearing it aloud made her even more fearful. He was just pretending, and at her insistence that he do so.

"Well, why look so stricken?" Adam asked in the astringent voice of a brother who'd known her all her life. "He must like you or he wouldn't be courting with you."

She burst into tears, wailing, "I've done something *Baremlich*!"

Her brother pulled her down next to him on hay bale that sat in the alley way between the rows of stalls. His voice bracing as he put an arm around her, Adam said, "Calm down now. Don't make a big deal of whatever this is. I'm sure you haven't really done anything terrible."

Burying her face in her hands, Becca wailed, "It's all pretend! I made Saul pretend to court me. None of this is real!"

"What did you say?" Adam pulled her hands away from her face.

She swallowed, repeating in a small voice. "I made Saul pretend to court me."

"How, exactly, did you force him to do this—and why!"

Becca jumped to her feet, pacing the barn alley way. "It's Chloe Nissly! She always acts like she can get anything or anyone she wants!"

"And this has to do what with you forcing Saul to court you?" Her brother questioned her, his expression one of confusion.

"Oh, she was all braggy, setting her sights on Thad Oberholtzer and I thought if I had a *Mann* courting me, I might make Thad jealous and best Chloe, too." She sank back onto the haybale next to Adam. "I thought Thad would see me as desirable and reject Chloe to spend time with me."

"And Saul?"

At first, I forced Saul into pretending to court me because I couldn't think of anyone else. At least, that's why I thought I asked him."

"You're in love with Thad Oberholtzer?" Adam still looked confused.

"*Neh*," Becca admitted, saying in a small voice, "I-I love Saul."

With a deep breath, Adam shook his head. "I don't understand any of this. Again, how did you force Saul to do anything he didn't want to do."

In a very small voice, she said, "I threatened to expose his having slashed the *Englischer's* tires."

"What?" Adam exploded. "Tell me that you did not use something I told you—in strictest confidence—to threaten Saul!"

"I'm sorry," Becca rushed to say. "I shouldn't have done it. I know that."

"You're darn right you shouldn't have done it! Why should I ever tell you anything again? Why should I not expose you to everyone as untrustworthy and a gossip?"

"There is no reason you shouldn't," she said in a sad voice. "I deserve that and more."

"You sure do," Adam said more calmly. "I love you. You're my sister, of course, I love you, but you shouldn't have done this."

"It wasn't, at all, sensible," she admitted. "It was a stupid idea and nothing matters now because I don't care about Thad or Chloe. I'm in love with Saul, who dislikes me and has reason to feel this way. We spend time together, but only because I forced him into it!"

Her brother took her hand. "I think you'd better tell me everything."

Tears welled up again in Becca's eyes and started rolling down her cheeks. "Yes."

Two days later, Becca pulled a tray of freshly baked cookies from the B & B oven and set them aside to return to the stove. She was missing a Sing at the Bricker *Haus* to help cook for this hastily-arranged party. While she hated missing the get-together, she dreaded talking to Saul, but she knew she must.

She had to release him from this stupid pretense of courting.

Having run into him a day before at the Offenhaler's store, just after learning she'd miss the Sing, she was relieved that she didn't yet have to worry about letting him know not to come to the *Haus* to get her. He didn't seem terribly upset that she couldn't come to the Sing, but it was hard to tell with him. His feelings were rarely visible.

Becca hoped her own weren't.

Just the sight of his broad shoulders and his impassive expression made her gulp and wish so much that he'd really chosen to court with her, that he was actually interested in her.

The pantry-kiss aside, she couldn't convince herself that he was doing any more than pretending to avoid exposure.

Closing her eyes, she sent up a prayer, *Please, Gott, if it is in your plan, let me somehow win Saul's affections. I know I have done many things I shouldn't have and You love me still. If I can only have one thing on this earth, I wish Saul to forgive me and see me as a possible Frau.*

Certainly, Saul seemed worth all her distress over him.

She had to think about this. She had to find the right moment to—to release him from pretending to court her. Somehow, she had to do this. Sometime soon.

"Why, *hallo* there," Chloe said in a smug tone two weeks later, walking up to Becca after the sermon the following Sunday.

"*Hallo,*" Becca responded without enthusiasm. Just now, she was heading back into the kitchen to check on the biscuits she'd put into oven five minutes before and she didn't really want to chitchat with Chloe.

She hadn't been able to tell Saul how she felt or that he was released from the pretend courtship. This needed to be done, though. She thought she ought to do it that day. Waiting was only making her more nervous.

Falling into step beside Becca, Chloe said, "We missed you at the Sing at the Bricker's *Haus* two weeks ago. It was very enjoyable. Did Adam mention that Saul sat next to me? He has a nice voice and we had such a fun time between the hymns."

Hearing a snide, triumphant note in the other girl's voice, Becca stopped. Before she thought about it, she demanded, "Why are you telling me this?"

106

Chloe shrugged, "No reason in particular. Just that we had a very nice time."

Her mouth quirking to one side, Becca said, "Good for you."

The girl just wasn't as important to her as she once was. Becca supposed she'd lately moved past feeling competitive with Chloe. It just didn't matter anymore.

She turned back to continue toward the kitchen.

"I think it wouldn't have been as much fun if I hadn't gotten to know Saul so much better," Chloe said in her irritating, self-satisfied voice.

Becca turned back looking at her with a shiver of chill running up her spine.

Moving forward with a flouncing of her skirt, Chloe said in the same satisfied voice, "Saul's a *Mann*. You know, not a *Buwe* like the others. I suppose it's because he's been head of his *familye* after his father died."

Becca's shiver shifted to a chill that ran right through her. She might not have any real claim on Saul, but the thought of him in another *Maedel's* clutches left her breathless, like she'd been thrown to the ground.

She didn't like the idea of him with any *Maedel*, but particularly not conniving Chloe Nissley.

"I thought you were interested in Thad," she said through numb lips.

Again, Chloe shrugged. "He's alright, I suppose, and he'll inherit his *Daed's* business, but he'll have to share it with his *Bruders*. Saul's an attractive *Mann* with a farm of his own."

She smiled in a way that left Becca's stomach turning. "Besides, Saul's got that husky voice and a face that isn't easily read. It makes him more interesting."

"He's…very interesting." Becca knew saying more would just increase Chloe's competitive nature.

"I know you've been spending time with Saul. Driving out with him." The other girl smiled at her. "You must see a lot of each other when he visits Adam. I know he's your brother's good friend.

Becca drew in a breath. Chloe's inference was clear as day and, while Becca wanted to dispute this, she paused. Hadn't she bullied Saul into helping her because he was so close at hand?

When she said nothing, Chloe went on. "I was so delighted when Saul was attentive at the Bricker's Sing and then when he asked to drive me home! Well, you can imagine how quickly I said yes."

Becca felt her heart had stopped. "Saul drove you home from the Sing?"

He'd driven Cloe home? What? Even when she'd always told him the girl's nature?

Becca suddenly felt the back of her neck start to heat.

Why would Saul drive Chloe home? Was he courting Chloe now?

"*Yah*," Chloe said with a dimpled smile. "It was so lovely and such a surprise! We had a wonderful ride."

Unable to speak, irritation running through her at the thought of Saul and Chloe, Becca stood in front of her, the hum of their friends and family in the yard loud around them.

Maybe it was just loud in her ears.

"You didn't know?" Chloe's face was even more triumphant. "I was so pleased to find he's as interested in me as I was in him. I guess he's not found another *Maedel* he likes as much as me. At least, that's what he said."

Saul actually said that to her!?

Becca considered for a moment smacking the silly girl and then finding Saul to smack him silly. She was kept from these very unkind acts by the fact that she couldn't move. Annoyance held her locked in place and some rational part of her told Becca that this was good.

She drew in another long breath, trying to wrestle her anger into a kinder, gentler emotion. What had Saul been thinking? Had he been interested in Chloe all the time Becca had been talking bad about the girl?

That Sunday afternoon, Saul went out to the fields, the late summer wind blowing around him. He'd missed the sermon this morning, having stayed home with his sick *Bruder*. Thank *Gott*, Gabe wasn't as upset to his stomach now and could sleep some. The night before had been bad.

The sun was setting on their day of rest—not that farmers ever got a day off. He felt, though, the need to check again on this acreage. It had lain fallow for a year or two and he'd just now bought the field off aged Joseph Beechy, who'd decided to go live near his sons. The land would make a nice addition to his own farm, if he didn't give it to Gabe, eventually.

Saul drew in a long, satisfied breath, looking over his land.

He didn't mind the solitary lull, the wind whistling softly through weeds that had grown in the untilled land

A scuffling sound behind him a few minutes later brought his head around and Saul saw the *kapped* figure of Becca just as she launched at him, her long gray skirts billowed out around her.

Saul staggered a little, the thrust of her slight weight having pushed him several feet back. "What the heck?! Are you crazy, *Maedel*? Where did you come from anyway?"

"How could you?! Just when I was starting to feel bad for you!"

Fending off her continued shoves as she yelled, he flipped her around, holding her hands in his, her backside pressed against the front of him.

"Becca! What's the matter with you? How did you even know I was here?"

"How could you?" She raged, not answering his question. "How could you when I told you about her? Were you just pretending all this time? Have you just been waiting your chance to court with Chloe?"

"What!" He felt the rise and fall of her rapid, angry breathing as he held her close, her full skirt flapping against his pants. It was no longer important how she'd known where to find him. He'd probably mentioned to Adam that he planned to check on the field.

"You heard me!" she raged.

Saul let her go then, as she'd stopped struggling to free herself, but he glared at her and braced himself for another onslaught. "Chloe? Did you say something about Chloe?"

Becca didn't launch herself at him again, however. She stood in front of him, spitting out the words, "Like you didn't hear me. You should have heard her bragging how you sat with her at the Sing. That you drove her home afterwards. How the two of you are courting now!"

"What are you talking about? I'm not courting Chloe Nissly. I never asked her to court." He tried to use his most level voice. "I'm not seeing her."

She just smirked at him.

"I never asked Chloe to court with me!" He repeated his words.

Becca gave him a murderous scowl. "You told her that you've just been driving out with me because I'm Adam's *Schweschder* and he sometimes needs you to cart me around! "That you haven't found a *Maedel* you like!"

"I never said any such thing." He knew this was all nonsense, but her words annoyed him all the same. "Of course, you're Adam's sister. Chloe knows that."

"Ohhh!!! Chloe!!!!" Becca mocked in a venomous voice.

He gave as sardonic a look as he could manage, saying sarcastically. "You sound very grown up now."

"You broke our agreement, Saul Stutzman!" Her cheeks were red as she shouted. "I could tell everyone about what you did to the *Englischer's* tires!"

"I did not break our agreement," he returned, just as angry, "and I can't believe you think I'm making up to Chloe Nissley. I've never been impressed with her. You're the one all snagged up on besting her!"

She thrust a hand to her hip, saying with a withering stare, "Are you saying you didn't drive her home from the last Sing?

That you didn't sit next to her all that evening? Are you claiming she made that up, too?"

"I'm not saying she made it up. I sat in the living room at the Sing and I suppose no one sat between us," Saul shot back. "Everyone was crowded in the *Haus*. And as for my driving her, she claimed she didn't have a way home, so I drove her home."

"You did! You admit it!"

"*Yah*, I admit it. I took a woman of our faith home to her parents." The words felt like dirt in his mouth and he dropped them out, his tone withering. "I don't know what Chloe said, but we're not courting. If I wanted to court with her—or anyone else—I'd have said so."

The heat seemed to have left her and Becca just looked at him with large, wet eyes.

His chest still hot and his stomach now as rebellious as his poor brother's had probably felt, Saul responded angrily, "And as for our agreement, I consider it at an end. You can tell whoever about the *Englischer's* tires. You always could have. I don't care."

With that, he turned back and climbed up on his farm wagon, heading back home.

Driving away from the field, his head buzzed with angry words he could have said to Becca, the image in his mind's eye of her standing alone in the field as he drove away.

How could she accuse him of courting with a woman she so despised? The thought ate at him and Saul's chest burned at the indictment.

...

CHAPTER TEN

Two days later, Saul leaned on the picket fence around the B & B, waiting for Becca to arrive at work.

After thinking and praying about the situation, Saul had calmed down some. He still didn't like her having assumed that he'd fallen for Chloe's tricks, but he guessed he could have tried harder to explain the truth to Becca.

There was no doubt she was very upset.

The cool early morning air felt fresh and soon the weather would become cooler. For a moment, Saul pondered on the reason behind Becca's anger with him. She'd been competitive with Chloe, but he hoped this was more. Stupid of him to have become attached to such a silly *Maedel*. He should just continue to address his *familye's* needs and stop thinking about Becca.

Just then, a black buggy drove around the corner, pulling to a stop in front of the B & B gate several feet away from Saul.

He straightened, seeing Adam behind the reins and Becca on the buggy seat beside her *Bruder*.

Saul swallowed as he waited for her to climb down from her seat. It was ridiculous to feel nervous about this, but he did.

From the buggy seat, Adam grimaced at him, a gesture that didn't make Saul feel any better about his potential reception. It was stupid, as he had as much reason to be angry with her as she did with him, more actually, since he'd never even thought of seeing Chloe romantically.

He certainly hadn't ever kissed her the way he'd done with Becca in the B & B pantry.

Standing on the other side of the buggy, Becca shook out her skirts. She then stepped around the back of the vehicle, her face stony. He'd never seen her that way. She didn't even look like herself. Becca kept her eyes averted, not meeting Saul's gaze.

"*Goedemorgen*, Becca," he said, holding the gate open for her.

To his irritation, she moved right past him—still not looking up at him—as if the gate had opened itself.

"Becca!"

The crazy *Maedel* sailed up the walk to the B & B front door, through which she whisked, completely ignoring Saul. He stared after her, not able to believe it. Even when he'd only been Adam's friend, she'd always had a smart remark for him.

"I tried to warn you," Adam said glumly from the buggy.

"How!? I didn't hear you say anything," Saul exploded, still surprised that Becca hadn't even responded to his presence. Although he'd been holding the gate open as he stared after her in shock, he let it go now.

"What did you think my expression meant?" Adam asked. "She's still all mad at you for making up to Chloe."

"I didn't make up to Chloe!" Saul shot back angrily.

"But you did drive her home after the Sing, didn't you? After sitting with her and making up to her?" His friend made another face at him.

"I did a service to another *Amishe* person. Is that a crime?" Saul threw over his shoulder as he stalked to where he'd left his own buggy.

"It's not a crime, friend, but your doing so certainly fired up my sister," Adam called after him.

"Your sister is crazy!" Saul put his foot on the step of his buggy, vaulting himself onto the seat before he grabbed the reins.

Becca leaned back against the closed B & B door behind her, tears streaming down her face, her hand stuffed in her mouth to stifle the sound of her sobs. She was angry at Saul and at herself, for caring about him and Chloe. She gulped in a sob, her chest heaving as she tried to stop. This was stupid. She didn't need to let him matter, at all. She had to get back to her life and stop thinking of Saul or Chloe or Thad. That *Mann* could look after himself and if Chloe snared him, Thad had only himself to blame.

Saul had only himself to blame for she'd told him about Chloe.

Although Adam had advocated for his friend as he drove her to work, she'd have expected nothing less. That didn't mean she believed Saul's story.

She'd prayed and prayed, trying to settle the turmoil in her chest, telling herself that *Gott* loved her, even if Saul didn't.

"...and he's courting Chloe now!" That evening, Becca stood—hands angrily at her waist--at the kitchen counter, supposedly helping Abby make dinner for the *familye*.

"Here. Slice these." Her sister plopped a leafy cluster of beets on the kitchen counter in front of Becca, not markedly moved by her furious outburst.

Looking at the root vegetables for a moment, she glared at them, saying, "I can't believe that after all I told him about Chloe—and her chasing after Thad because of their family store— that Saul is actually courting her now! He wants to marry her!"

"He said that?" Abby looked up from the pot she was stirring.

"Well, he drove her home from the Sing last week! Did I tell you that?"

"*Yah*," Abigail responded, still stirring. "Saul actually told you he's courting with Chloe—you know this kind of thing isn't talked about—and said that he wants to marry her?"

"He didn't have to tell me!" Becca stormed, wiping at her wet cheek with the back of one hand. She couldn't seem to stop crying about this. Saul wasn't worth it! "He admitted to my face that he'd sat next to Chloe at the Sing and that he'd driven her home in his buggy."

Abby stared at her, a wrinkle between her brows. "Drove her home? And he had an understanding with you? He has been driving you out a lot, sister—which surprised me some—but you know that a few buggy drives doesn't mean the two of you will marry."

"I know that," Becca snapped.

Her *Schweschder* lifted her hand. "Hey, no need to get upset with me. Are you done with the beets?"

Becca had washed them in the sink, but the red vegetables still sat on the counter in front of her with the leafy greens still attached. She sliced into them, answering her sister, "Not yet, and I'm not upset at you...just upset in general."

"So, you and Saul had an understanding, but he drove Chloe home from the Sing?"

There were several moments of silence in the kitchen, Becca struggling with herself. Maybe it was time to be honest about her situation with Saul.

Looking at the red beets bleeding all over her hands as she cut into them, she confessed, "I haven't been totally honest about me and Saul. I—I do care about him, but he doesn't care at all about me."

"What do you mean? He took you out in his buggy more than once and he took you to eat with his *familye*. I don't see why he'd do that if he didn't have some feelings for you." Abby frowned, her fingers busily snapping stems off green beans in a bowl.

Becca rinsed a little beet juice off her hands before she scratched her neck, not wanting to admit to her sister that she'd essentially coerced Saul into making Thad—and more particularly, Chloe—jealous.

She swallowed.

"What do you mean?" Abby asked again, her hands stopping snapping the stems as she looked at her sister through squinting eyes. "What do you mean?"

Becca stiffened her spine, lifting her head to meet her sister's gaze. "I'm not proud of it, but I blackmailed Saul into helping me. Driving out with me…acting like we were courting."

"What! Blackmailed him? What do you mean?"

Becca hung her head, not able to meet Abigail's eyes. "I—I threatened him."

She looked up, saying in a voice that pleaded for understanding, "In the beginning, I just wanted him to help me, to act like he was interested in me, so Thad Oberholtzer would see me as a *Maedel* to—to court and maybe start acting…interested in me."

"Why?" Abby said, incredulity in her voice. "Why would you do this and how did you coerce—threaten—Saul?"

Choosing to answer the first question, Becca cleared her throat before she burst forth with, "Because of get-everything-she-wants Chloe Nissly, that's why!"

"What does Chloe have to do with this?" Her sister moved to sit down at the *familye* table, apparently feeling the conversation required her full attention.

Becca picked up a kitchen towel to dry off the hands she'd just again washed free of sticky beet juice. She slapped the damp towel down on the counter. "She's always winning at everything and she hinted to me that she was going after Thad because he'll inherit his father's store and, therefore, be a *gut* husband."

"Yes." Abby's voice was patient.

"And I thought Thad deserved better…and that Chloe shouldn't get everything, so I talked Saul into helping me make Thad jealous." Her voice dwindled as she spoke.

"You talked him into it?" Abby lifted her brows, clearly waiting for the full explanation she knew was behind this.

"If you must know," Becca burst out, "I threatened to tell everyone something he didn't want others knowing. Adam—Adam told me. Our *Bruder* told me because he thought he could trust me not to say anything."

She swallowed. "I realize it was stupid and that I broke Adam's trust. I'm very sorry about it now, but Saul's a cheater and a liar! He told me he'd help me make Thad jealous, so Thad pursued me, not Chloe!"

"And he kissed me!" she ended on a wail.

"Thad kissed you?" Abby was, as usual, determined to get all the facts.

Becca quietened. "No. Saul kissed me. In the B & B pantry that time we were hiding there from Chloe seeing me covered in cherry juice."

"You don't need to tell me whatever Saul doesn't want spread around," Abigail reminded her. "Let's not make your transgression any worse. I only know anything about this because you told me a little of it and I certainly didn't know why you and Saul were in the pantry. He kissed you in there? And Adam told you about this secret of Saul's in the beginning?"

Abby was clearly trying to make sense of Becca's mess.

"*Yah*. Because he told Adam and Adam later told me," Becca responded in a small voice.

Her *Schweschder* said, "So, you not only blackmailed Saul into helping you, you also broke Adam's trust?"

"Yes!" Becca admitted, "and I feel very bad about both, but Saul turned out to be a *Schlang*! He'd deserve it if I did tell everyone—his whatever!"

"Saul's not a snake. Remember, he's the same *Mann* you kissed in the B & B pantry. I still don't know why the two of you were there together. That was when you were covered with cherry juice and he saved you from being seen by Chloe and Thad."

"He kissed me! I didn't kiss him," she felt the need to insert. "At least, I wasn't the one who started the kissing."

"He's Adam's best friend," Abigail continued as if she hadn't spoken, "and...and you're not gossiping to anyone. We don't gossip about our neighbors. Remember?"

"I should," Becca said viciously. Just the thought of Saul and Chloe together hurt her deep in her soul. "I won't though. I'm better than him."

Abby smiled. "Okay."

"Anyway, Adam told me about what had happened when Saul did—oh, heck. He slashed an *Englischer's* tires after the *Englisher* drove crazy in his car and knocked Leah over. Saul himself told me all about it." Becca shrugged. "She was just hurt, but the *Englischer* could have killed her."

"Oh."

"The whole thing happened years ago when Saul and Leah were younger and he was really upset about what had happened to his sister." Becca drew in and released a deep breath. "He's always kind to his *familye*."

Abigail shrugged. "It sounds like he was kind to you, too."

"*Yah*," Becca said, hoping she didn't sound as forlorn as she felt. "Right up to the point that he started courting Chloe. He's a *schlang*, I tell you."

"Becca's crazy!" Saul told Adam the next day, the two of them taking a break in the shade of Saul's corn harvesting machine. Autumn was coming, but the sun shone warm on them.

"She's *narrish*! You saw the way she walked right past me at the B & B!"

None of their farm workers were free. If Abe and Ben hadn't been working another field and young Gabe helping their *Mamm*, Saul would have had to harvest the field himself. Thankfully, Adam had been free to help.

"*Yah*, I did," he said with a grin.

Adam didn't seem to get the full picture of his sister's behavior. Saul thought with frustration, he actually seemed amused by the whole situation.

"She's not crazy," her brother said. "She's just really upset with you."

"No kidding." Saul stared a moment at the dirt in front of him. "I ought to give you a thrashing for telling her about the *Englischer's* tires."

That sobered Adam up. "You ought to and if you want to take a shot at me, I've got it coming. I never thought she'd tell anyone or use the story to threaten you, I promise. I've told Becca how disappointed I am in her."

"I'm not going to take a shot at you." Saul didn't want to hit his friend and he knew it wasn't what *Gott* would want, either.

As irritated as he was that knowledge of his foolish action had gotten around to Becca, he'd had some time to come to terms with his friend's lapse in judgment.

He supposed Becca would spread that story around, now that he'd angered her, Saul thought grimly.

"If I'm honest," he said slowly, "I never was worried about others hearing about that situation."

Adam looked at him for a moment. "Then why did you get into this spot with Becca? She said she blackmailed you into acting like you two were together This doesn't sound like you."

Saul took a deep breath before saying, "I don't know. I don't know why I did it."

He shrugged. "I never cared what others heard. I made my peace with *Gott* about that long ago."

"Becca was all worried that Chloe was after Thad and wanted to get him interested in herself." Saul stopped. "I just decided to help her. Do her a favor."

He fell silent.

"I know." Adam looked at him again. "She told me about Chloe and Thad when she admitted what she'd done. She apologized for what she did with you. She owed me an apology. She's never told anyone stuff I say to her. My *Schweschder* usually keeps whatever secrets I tell her."

Saul absently scuffed his foot in the dirt. "I guess I didn't want…. I didn't like the idea of her getting with Thad…or asking some other *Mann* to pretend to court her, like I did. You wouldn't have wanted her to do such a thing!"

Silence beat between them for a few minutes.

"I didn't really think it out," Saul admitted.

"Oh," said Becca's brother.

Saul drew in another long breath. "I don't know."

"So," Adam said slowly, "you didn't agree to Becca's plan because her threat scared you."

"No."

"Then, it seems to me that you'd better figure out exactly why you did go along with this."

Saul dropped his gaze to the dirt again. It didn't pay to think about why he'd done this. Everything with Becca was messed up now.

"Saul is such an upstanding *Mann*," Chloe sighed. "He seems so different than the other *Menner* with whom I've driven out. So careful of his *familye* and so honest."

With their church members and friends milling around her and Saul's new *Maedel* having plopped down in the chair beside her before the next service, Becca had the thought rush through her that this was the time to expose him. This was the moment to tattle on him.

All she had to do was tell Chloe about him having slashed the *Englischer's* tires and the girl would manage to spread the word around, even though they were directed not to gossip about their brethren. Chloe would see that she didn't really know Saul.

Not really.

The words clogged in Becca' throat, though. She wouldn't expose Saul's secret. Instead, she said, without enthusiasm, "*Hallo,* Chloe."

"*Hallo,*" Chloe returned, clearly pleased with herself.

To be fair, she always looked pleased with herself, but Becca was pretty sure the girl's smirk had to do with getting Saul's attention.

She should tell Chloe about Saul's sordid secret. She knew she should—just to spite him—but she couldn't.

She still loved Saul, stupid as it was, and his actions weren't her business. Not what he'd done with the *Englischer's* tires, anyway. She'd resisted telling Abby about it and had only done so at the end because she knew her sister would never spread it to others, if only to respect Adam more than she had.

Looking blindly to the side, as if she was perusing the Miller's main living room, she averted her face from Chloe. Becca knew her expression was too easily read and she didn't want to add to Chloe's gloating.

No matter how hard she tried, Becca couldn't stop loving Saul and she'd tried everything. She reminded herself of his betrayal and, in a further dig at her already tearful feelings, told herself again that Saul had never truly loved her. He'd only been pretending, and that, only at her pushing.

Lots of *Menner* kissed *Maedels*…probably in kitchen pantries. It didn't mean anything and she definitely had to stop thinking about that episode. She'd been kissed by *Menner* before.

Becca looked off to the side again, distressed that tears prickled behind her eyes.

To her frustration, Chloe wiggled in the chair beside her, as if settling in.

Becca could have burst into tears.

It was, at least, half an hour before the meeting was to begin. The Zook *familye* didn't usually come this early, but Becca's *Mamm* had wanted to bring several casseroles for the lunch afterwards. She'd made them to serve with everything else after the service and Becca had agreed to come with her *Mamm*, the casserole dishes warm on her lap in the jiggling buggy.

She'd never wished so fiercely that a church service would start early.

Chloe said in a chatty voice, "The air was so chilly when Saul drove me that he had to offer me his jacket."

The girl giggled. "It was so big on me. Saul is a very muscular young *Mann*."

"*Yah*." She didn't want to hear this.

Becca usually enjoyed the time before a meeting, visiting her friends, young children running around before finding seats. Young *Frau* sitting, chatting with *Bopplin* on their knees. The noise of chatter around the two of them increased, but she had no interest in talking to anyone.

Least of all the *Maedel* at her side.

Now, all she could do was sit next to her tormentor, her stomach twisting sick inside her.

"It never seemed so fast to get to my *Haus* as it did that night," Chloe said with another giggle. "I so enjoyed being with Saul that the time just raced past. He's such a wonderful buggy driver. So safe."

Impelled by her misery and bitter to her bones, Becca felt the words to expose him choke in her throat, but she still held her tongue. She could easily have retaliated—against the shallow bully beside her and against Saul, who hadn't upheld his part of their foolish bargain. His courting with Chloe had definitely broken their agreement! But Becca didn't say anything. She wouldn't. She knew now why the young Saul had acted the way he had and she couldn't bring herself to chatter about it.

Whatever he'd done was between himself and *Gott* and she had nothing to say about it.

CHAPTER ELEVEN

The week after church service, Saul paused, climbing down to take off his broad hat, having plowed a fallow field. He wiped the dampness off his forehead. Even though the wind blew cooler than the heat at the first of August, he'd worked up sweat, holding the plow straight while directing his team of horses.

He'd spent the last few days mulling over his situation with Becca. He'd always known her. She was Adam's annoying little *Schweschder. Yah*, his friend was older than all, but one of his five sisters. Yet, only Becca had ever been this annoying.

He hadn't agreed to her ridiculous scheme because he was afraid of having his sins exposed. He'd talked to Bishop Wagmann about that several years before. He wasn't sure exactly why he'd agreed to help her. She was his friend's sister. Weren't they to help others?

Not given to spending his time examining his internal thoughts, Saul had found the last few weeks to be awkward and uncomfortable. Adam had recommended that Saul figure out why he'd engaged in this pretense with Becca. A good idea, no doubt.

Saul sighed.

Staring off in the distance toward the tree line that grew between the fields, he admitted to himself that he'd gotten into this mess without reaching out to *Gott* to find the best path. He should have prayed about getting involved in Becca's plan, but he'd fallen into the pattern of thinking his dilemmas weren't big enough to bother *Gott*.

Foolish when *Gott* had his eye on even the smallest bird.

As stumped as he felt now, prayer was his most obvious recourse.

Dear Gott,

What do I do now? I got into this mess with Becca and, now that she's all mad at me, I don't know how to get out. I've tried talking to her, but she won't even let me explain. You know that Chloe means nothing to me, but I haven't even been given the chance to explain that to Becca. Please, help me know what to do now.

Amen

Shoving his sweat-damp hat back on his head, Saul got back up in the plow seat and chucked to his team to move. The horses would be thirsty now, even though the weather wasn't hot.

As he drove them slowly back to the barn, he only hoped he could hear *Gott's* direction. It was always his prayer to hear what he needed to hear, but he didn't think he'd ever before felt this alone, even though he was driving back to a farmhouse that provided shelter for seven.

"I really screwed everything up," Becca sadly told Adam several days later. "In the beginning, I thought this whole thing would be a way to help Thad and—and to show Chloe she can't have everything, but apparently she can! Now, she even has Saul. Perhaps I was right to think of Thad, after all."

"Don't be ridiculous," her brother said.

She heaved a deep sigh, going on as if he hadn't spoken. "I was wrong. I don't even care about Thad anymore. If he's silly enough to let Chloe catch him, then she can have him. Although, Chloe's now courting with another *Mann.* Saul! How could he?"

Adam leaned against the foot of her bed, lounging there beside her. "Is that why you got into this situation? Really? Because of Chloe and Thad? You dragged Saul into it—using a secret that I shared in confidence with you—and you threatened him. Saul! Of all people to threaten. He's so tough and I'd never think he could be pushed into this pretense, but you went right after him."

Becca felt a tear track down her cheek. She'd told herself she wouldn't cry over Saul anymore, but she hadn't been able to keep this promise to herself. It didn't look like she was very *gut* at keeping promises. Actually, she didn't feel very good at anything about now.

"You really care about him, don't you?" Adam's dark eyes watched her.

Breaking out in a wail, she sobbed, "I love him! I know he's a jerk and he's with Chloe now, but I love him."

"Don't be stupid," her brother recommended, using a stronger word this time. "I don't know much about all this, but I'll be very surprised if he's truly with her."

Becca hiccupped, trying to squelch her sobs. "What makes you say that? Of course, he is! He admitted it and she bragged about it."

"*Neh*, Saul said he sat near her at the Sing and then drove her home that night. That doesn't mean he's courting her. I know this because Saul's not foolish. He *schmaert* and tough. I just can't see him with Chloe. She's a lightweight."

Refusing to be consoled, Becca sniffled and said, "Saul admitted it to me!"

Adam just shook his head. "You don't know the whole story and you won't even talk to him. What's Saul supposed to do?"

"You said it yourself, *Bruder*. Saul's smart and tough. If I hadn't gotten it right, he'd find a way to tell me. I-I just don't need to hear from his mouth anymore about him courting Chloe."

"But, you're still in love with him?"

"I am," she admitted, "but I'm praying to *Gott* to help me get over it."

Adam shrugged. "It might be good to pray for the best outcome. That would give *Gott* leeway in answering your prayers. After all, that's what you want."

"When is that sweet Becca Zook coming to dinner again?" Saul's *Mamm* asked later that evening. She stood stirring a pot on the stove, while Saul sat at the *familye* table in the kitchen across from her.

"I don't know," he responded flatly, looking down at the boiled potatoes he was mashing for her.

His mother stopped stirring to turn toward him. "How is this? You can ask her, can't you? Then you would know."

"I can ask," he said, "but I doubt she'll come."

"The two of you are in a fight?" Susanna Stutzman asked.

Saul took a moment to answer, steadily stirring the now mashed potatoes.

"Stop that," his *Mamm* reproached. "You'll have them turning to glue. Tell me, have you gotten crosswise with Becca?"

An ironic smile quirked his mouth. "Why would you say that?"

"Because we haven't seen her in a while and I know you!"

"I'm not a quarrelsome *Mann*," he said.

"*Neh*, but you can be stubborn," Susanna observed. "And that can be more of a problem than being quarrelsome. Are you in a fight with Becca?"

Saul released a deep breath. "*Yah*, I guess so, but I never meant to be."

"Have you tried talking with her?"

"Of course," he said impatiently, "but she won't even give me a chance to explain. Why should I have to work so hard to make her see reason? I was doing her a favor and now she's all mad at me? The girl makes me *narrish*."

His mother smiled. "You're definitely not crazy, son. Just pig-headed sometimes. I think you probably need to try again to talk to Becca."

Saul took a deep breath, removing his sweaty broad-brimmed hat as he walked into the Oberholtzer feedstore the next day,. He'd thought a lot about it, deciding this was the right thing to do. As crazy as it seemed, he was doing this for Becca.

The building was cool and dim, shafts of light hitting the grain dust hanging in the air. Several customers stood at the counter where Thad Oberholtzer's brother, Reuben, worked.

Waiting until Reuben Oberholtzer was finished serving the men ahead of him, Saul gazed around the building, swinging his hat as he occupied himself. As a farmer, feedstores were always interesting.

His stomach didn't feel happy, though. Saul registered this, wandering with his unseeing gaze resting on the first row of shelves. He'd been mulling the situation over since Becca sailed right past him at the B & B that morning.

The whole mess weighed on him and it bothered him that she'd never even heard him out. Apparently, she wasn't going to listen to his side of things, however.

"Can I help you?" Having finished with the others ahead of Saul, Reuben Oberholtzer spoke to him.

His jaw firm, Saul turned. "Is your brother Thad here? I need to speak to him."

"*Yah*," answered Reuben without much interest. "He's back in the storeroom. I'll get him for you."

Feeling determined—and a little foolish—at the same time, Saul stood waiting at the counter, knowing he was doing the right thing. Becca had asked his help, in her own contrary way. She was silly and wrong about him and Chloe, but Saul still felt obligated. It might not make sense to him—and was, in fact, the opposite of what he wanted, but she'd wanted this door open.

He could at least do this. He tapped his hat against his thigh.

The curtain that blocked the storeroom off from the area behind the counter parted a few minutes after Reuben had disappeared behind it and Thad Oberholtzer appeared.

"*Goedemorgen*. You wanted to speak with me?"

For an instant, Saul looked upon the face of the *Mann* that Becca had tried to take from Chloe.

Smiling at Saul mildly, Thad didn't look like the prize the two girls seemed to think he was, but a husband was a husband and, at least, the *Mann* looked to have a future here at the feedstore.

"If you have a minute, I'd like to speak with you."

"Of course." Thad Oberholtzer waited.

Feeling this was better said without the chance of them being overheard, Saul nodded to the end of the counter, away from where Reuben stood. "Could we step over here?"

"Of course," Thad said again, a glimmer of uneasiness crossing his bland features as he moved to the end of the counter.

Saul knew he had to get quickly to the point, as he didn't want to be here, at all. Hat dangling from his hand, he said, "You know Becca Zook."

It was a statement. Everyone in their small community knew the Zook *familye*.

"*Yah*, of course." Thad nodded as he said the words for the third time.

"I've been friends with Adam Zook for years and have known Becca all her life."

Thad nodded again, but said nothing this time. He just cast a look toward his *Bruder*, as if he'd done something wrong and was about to get scolded by Saul.

Unclear as to how he could have scolded the other *Mann*, Saul took another deep breath and then said with resolve. "I just wanted to say that Becca Zook is a good *Maedel*. Worth a score of other girls. Certainly, more honest than…some that might have been making up to you. I've spent a lot of time with her and…I just think you should know this about Becca."

Thad looked confused. "*Denki*. I do know that Adam Zook has been your friend for years. I'm not sure why you're talking to me about his sister, though. Of course, I know Becca. We all went to school together and have worshiped together. *Yah*, I know her."

Saul wondered what Becca saw in this *Mann* to have drawn her attention. Thad looked spiritless and ordinary to him.

Of course, he was not to judge his brethren, but still.

A few seconds passed, Thad blinking at him in confusion. "Haven't you been driving out with Becca? I'm confused. I thought I saw you driving her home after the last Sing."

Saul nearly snorted. That was what started all this with Becca, her anger at his having driven Chloe home after that gathering and here Thad—the focus of Becca's attention—didn't even recognize the difference between Cloe and Becca. He couldn't see himself making the same mistake.

Finding he had to steel himself, Saul shifted the brim of his hat in his hand and said tersely, "I just wanted you to know—since Becca and I have spent more time together recently—that she's a *gut* girl. A really outstanding *Maedel*. She'll make the right *Mann* a good *Frau*."

Thad smiled without rancor. "Of course, she is or you wouldn't have spent all that time with her."

Lifting his gaze to stare the other *Mann* straight in the eyes, Saul said, "Becca and I aren't courting."

"Oh." Thad looked mystified, as if not clear on why Saul made such a blunt statement. Particularly since such things weren't matters for public consideration. "Okay. Of course…this kind of thing wouldn't be discussed."

"I'm discussing it." Saul didn't even try to dress it up. "I'm telling you I have no understanding with Becca or with Chloe Nissley, for that matter."

"Chloe Nissley?" Thad looked as if he was completely baffled by their conversation.

"*Yah*, you have been driving around with Chloe recently." Saul couldn't keep the scorn out of his comment.

"Yes, we have taken some buggy drives together, Chloe and I." Thad still looked bewildered.

"Well," Saul said, shifting his hat again, "I just wanted you to know that Becca isn't promised to me. She'd make a good wife and that she's not courting with me."

With those words, he turned on his heel and stalked out of the feedstore. He didn't want to get in her way or keep her from doing as she wished.

Even if that meant her marrying Thad Oberholtzer.

CHAPTER TWELVE

The truth was staring him in the face, Saul thought a day later as he sat alone in the living room of their *Haus* before supper. He had to admit it, at least to himself.

He loved Becca Zook. He'd even—foolishly—recommended her to Thad, even though Saul wanted her for himself.

Silly, wonderful Becca.

He'd been thinking about this for days and he couldn't any longer deny to himself that he'd developed feelings for Adam's little sister. Of course, she'd now get with Thad. Saul had almost assured that, but he'd done it for Becca.

That was what she wanted. Had wanted from the beginning.

The cheerful voices of his *familye* members could be heard in the kitchen and he knew that Gabe would soon come in after caring for the animals.

Saul brooded, his gaze not registering anything as he considered how badly he wished Becca would again smile at him.

"*Hallo, Bruder,*" Leah said cheerfully, interrupting his thoughts.

He looked up as she flopped onto the couch next to him.

"I went to see Thad Oberholtzer yesterday," Saul announced immediately, gloom in his voice and no clear purpose in his mind.

"Okay." His sister looked at him, her eyes squinting as if she were trying to solve a puzzle. She echoed, "You went to see Thad Oberholtzer."

Even though Becca had reprimanded him about using a directive tone when he'd talked to Leah, his sister didn't seem to have any resentment toward him.

131

"I went to see him to tell him that Becca would be a *gut* wife."

"Okay," his Schweschder said again, this time more slowly. "Ummmm. Why would you do that, when you want to marry her yourself?"

Saul turned to look at her. How did Leah know this? Was he that easy to read? "What makes you think I want to marry her?"

Her comment startled him as he wasn't accustomed to others seeing beyond his non-expressive face.

"Please." Leah reached out to pat the hand he'd had resting on his knee. "Of course, you want to marry Becca, *Bruder*. Not only have you never before brought a *Maedel* here to meet us all, you're now making cow eyes and mooning all over the place. Of course, you're in love."

"What?! What do you mean, I've been mooning? Cow eyes?"

"Well, you are. Mooning." Leah wasn't even affected by his thunderous exclamation, sitting next to him with a comfortable expression.

He repeated explosively, "Cow eyes! Why I've never even talked about Becca!"

Leah just gave him a level glance. "You don't have an answer regarding your having brought her to dinner here, huh?"

Saul just scowled at his sister.

"Let's try this," Leah suggested, "Can you tell me that you don't care about Becca?"

He didn't let his expression change, but he couldn't—wouldn't—answer her question. Yes, he loved Becca, but there was no point in talking about it.

Leah just shrugged. "I haven't said anything before because you seemed to have the situation in hand, but now..."

"How do you know I don't have the situation in hand now?" he demanded.

"You just told me that you recommended Becca to Thad Oberholtzer," Leah reminded him. "I wouldn't have said anything otherwise. You normally handle everything very well. You're terrific at farming. You're making sure the boys all have farmland, which will allow our *familye* to all be together, and you've done

132

great at steering us all through dealing with *Daed* not being here. You suck at this Becca thing, though."

"Thank you," he said sarcastically.

"You're welcome." Leah stretched her arms out along the back of their couch. "Just ask if you want any help in sorting things out with her."

"How very kind of you," Saul responded in the same ironic tone. "I think I can manage, though."

"Okay," Leah said in a breezy tone, "but you're not doing very well so far."

Saul just stared at her. She was right, he acknowledged to himself. He wasn't doing very well with Becca.

Snapping cauliflower branches off the white vegetable as they readied the *familye* supper, Becca stood that day at the kitchen counter with her sister.

"I'm going to lie down on my bed for a short nap before supper," *Grossmammie* said, smacking a kiss on Becca's cheek, before she hobbled off toward the bedroom.

"I'll come get you to eat," Becca called after her grandmother, going back to the cauliflower in the bowl.

"You're very quiet," Abby observed after a few minutes of the two of them working steadily without talking.

Their *Mamm* and the three sisters nearest them in age were off helping a friend, so it was just the two girls alone in the kitchen. *Daed* and their *Bruders* were still out in the fields, while Faith, the youngest in the *familye* hadn't yet come in from school.

Becca looked over at her, putting a strained smile on her face. "I'm just focusing on getting our meal together."

"You've never before felt the need to do this in silence," Abby commented. "What's going on? You're very quiet recently. Is something on your mind?"

Looking at her elder sister, Becca paused. "I don't know. Nothing is going on, I guess. I've just been thinking--maybe I should actually court with Thad Oberholzer. I've no chance with Saul and Chloe can't have every *Mann*."

Why couldn't she get this right? Becca sent up a prayer to *Gott*. She had nothing specific to say. She just felt miserable.

"I'm twenty-years-old," she observed finally, "and I'm not even courting with a *Buwe*. What's wrong with me? You and Gabe were married by my age."

For a moment Abigail made no response and Becca closed her eyes briefly, kicking herself for having thoughtlessly brought up Abby's dead husband. Her sister never said much about her grief, but everyone knew this was why she'd not married again. It took time to get over a first love.

Abby cleared her throat. "*Yah*. I did marry early."

Becca said nothing.

"But you know, *Schweschder*, that doesn't mean I had a perfect marriage," Abby sliced the cabbage in front of her into thin slices, "or that I'm perfect. I sometimes think you believe this."

"Of course," Becca responded, in agony at her own thoughtlessness, "it wasn't perfect, Gabe died so young. I know you miss him."

Her sister was silent for a moment. "I do miss Gabe, but that doesn't mean I thought he was perfect. None of us are perfect."

"That is true," Becca said, still frustrated with herself for having even brought up her sister's marriage. "You knew Gabe like no one else. You were his wife. Of course, you saw his human frailties. His death was tragic, though. The two of you had just started out."

Abigail looked back down at the cabbage she was slicing, pausing to cup her hands around the slices to move them to a bowl that sat nearby. She lifted her chin then, saying, "Gabe and I were married more than three years. His death was tragic and, *yah*, we had just started out. I do miss him, still. That's not what I meant, though, about not being perfect. I meant me. I wasn't talking about Gabe."

Becca turned to look at her sister. Abigail Zook Eichelberger was the oldest Zook child and three years older than Becca.

"But...you are perfect or pretty close to it." There was really no denying this. Abigail had always seemed serene and had always done pretty much everything well.

Abby looked up at her. "Don't be foolish, Becca. It has to be obvious to everyone."

"What?" Becca stared at her in bewilderment.

Abby drew in a deep breath and then carefully laid aside the knife she'd been using.

Becca noticed then the finest tremble in her *Schweschder's* fingers.

"I failed my husband." Abby pushed away from the counter and went out to sit in the living room.

Startled to find her sister this upset—and surprised to see Abby opening up this way—she followed her into the living room to sit in the closest chair. "This is nonsense, Abby! How can you say that you failed Gabe?"

Abby gave her a withering look. "You said yourself that Gabe and I married young. That we'd been married over three years."

"*Yah?*"

"Isn't it obvious?"

"*Neh.* Not to me."

"Becca!" she said in a sharp tone that her sister had learned meant Abby was upset. "I have no child! Gabe and I had no children!"

Abby dropped her face into her hands.

Only once, Becca had heard that tone in her voice or had seen her sister cry. On that one childhood occasion, Abby had made a silly childhood mistake, dropping a basket of hen's eggs to make a messy puddle.

"Abby," Becca moved to lay a hand on her sister's shoulder. "This isn't a failure. Gabe died—"

"Childless," Abigail lifted her head to say. "Gabe died childless. I failed to give him a child in three. Long. Years. More than three years of marriage, actually. I wasn't even with child when he died."

Becca slipped an arm around her *Schweschder's* shoulders. "Three years isn't all that long. Just look at the Biblical story of Abraham and Sarah."

"Please," Abby said, using a nearby dish towel to scrub the tears off her cheeks, "I'm not Sarah."

"*Neh,* but you have no idea what God has intended. Gabe had an unfortunate accident. We know, that these things happen in this evil world, but *Gott* still has all power. He makes the choice of child or no child. There are women around us who've never married and some married without *Kinder*. Some with only one or two *Kinder*."

"I know, I know," Abigail said, "but Gabe and I were healthy. We should have had children."

"These things are not always visible," Becca retorted. "Just look at Frau Blinkersdorfer. She's the picture of health. No children after having been married twenty or so years."

"Yes," Abby said, scrubbed her cheeks dry and then returned her sister's hug with a squeeze. "I only mention the whole thing, dear Becca, because I've gradually come to realize you're comparing yourself to me. None of us are perfect. We here in this world compare ourselves. *Gott* never does. All are loved by Him."

Even Chloe, Becca realized grudgingly. *Gott* loved even mean-spirited Chloe.

Becca looked at her *Schweschder*. "I don't think the three years you and Gabe were married—"

"Three and a half," Abigail inserted. "You heard what I heard! Even Gabe's friends knew he was disappointed!"

"Fine. Three and a half years. I still don't think that means for sure that you're like *Frau* Blinkersdorfer. And Gabe's friend may have said that mean thing about his not having children to carry on, but that doesn't mean Gabe felt that way."

"Maybe not," Abby said, "but I'm still not perfect."

"You seem pretty perfect to me," Becca muttered in a low voice.

"See?" Her sister said. "This is what I mean. You think you're supposed to be like me or like Chloe Nissley presents herself. *Gott* knows we are none of us perfect and He loves us still. I also think Saul loves you, but you're too blind to see it."

Becca drew in a sniffling breath. "You're wrong, Abby. You're not often wrong, but you are this time. I should probably try to court with Thad. At least, I may have a chance there."

"Don't be silly. Saul does care for you. It was obvious whenever he came to pick you up for drives," Abigail said with exasperation. "I don't think he'd have driven out so often with you, if he didn't care. Or teased you so often when he came to see Adam."

"It was all pretend," Becca reminded her, the words feeling like hard lumps in her throat. "I threatened him. I made him pretend to like me."

"Really?" Her *Schweschder* laughed. "I don't think Saul does anything he doesn't want to do. No matter what you said you'd do, he wouldn't scare easily. I believe he loves you."

"No," Becca sniffled again. "He's with Chloe now. You're wrong this once. I told you how I threatened him with the secret Adam told me. Saul doesn't care about me."

"Then why," asked her exasperated sister, "did he show up at the B & B that morning when Adam took you to work? And you wouldn't talk to him!"

Dropping her head, she said, "Saul knew I was upset with him…and that he'd totally broken our…agreement. He was probably there to try to talk me out of…doing what I'd threatened to do, that's all."

Abby shook her head. "You're wrong, Becca. I can't believe he cares about all that. I'm not sure he ever did. It doesn't sound like Saul."

"Of course, he worried about me talking!" Becca shot back. "Why else would he ever have agreed to help me? No, I'm convinced that he, somehow, fell for Chloe and I just need to get over him."

"Saul wants to talk to you. Please, listen to him. If just for me. You owe me, right," Adam said when they both sat on hay bales out by the barn. The sun was setting in the western sky as the day closed, leaving streaks of red, yellow and lavender melting into pink.

"It's alright," Becca said in a tight voice. "You can tell him not to worry. I'm not saying anything to anybody about the *Englischer's* tires."

Adam shook his head. "I don't think this has anything to do with that. "He just wants to talk with you."

Sighing, her mid-section hurting these past few days, as if she'd eaten a bunch of unripe plums, Becca knew with everything in her that she couldn't listen to Saul admit to her that he was in love with Chloe.

She got up to go inside, tears threatening.

"No, *Bruder*. Just tell him we have nothing to say to one another."

"*Hallo*, Becca."

Staring into Thad Oberholtzer's bland face two days later, she wondered how she'd ever thought she wanted him to see her as a possible *Frau*. She'd never been absolutely convinced that she wanted to marry Thad, but that seemed so far now from anything she'd ever chose, Becca could only look at him for a moment.

Realizing with a start that she hadn't responded to him, she stretched her mouth into something like a smile, saying, "*Hallo*."

Thad removed his broad straw had as he climbed the porch steps. "I realized I didn't see you at services last Sunday and I wanted to come say *hallo*."

"*Hallo*," she said again. "No, I don't believe I did see you there. I was there, though."

"Oh."

Her natural courtesy kicking in, Becca waved to the chairs that occupied the front porch, "Please, sit down."

It wasn't as if a *Buwe* had never come over to visit, but her heart having settled so totally on Saul, drove all courting behaviors right out of her mind.

She settled into the porch swing at a right angle to the chair he now occupied.

"I believe I saw you last when I was driving Chloe around on some errands. As I remember, she asked as her *Mamm* had their second buggy out that day."

He sounded so neutral in his offhand remark that Becca wondered if he'd ever had romantic interest in the other girl.

"*Yah*, I do believe that's when we met last."

"No!" Thad slapped his thigh. "I remember now! I saw you last when I drove Chloe here to your *Haus* that day. Her *Mamm* has their second buggy out quite a lot."

"Yes. I do remember that now, also." Becca tried not to sound as frustrated as she felt with herself. She knew her face was too readable. At the moment, she couldn't imagine she'd ever let herself get caught up in competing for anything with Chloe. It just seemed silly.

"I don't mind taking others around when they need it," he said.

Becca acknowledged to herself that Thad was a *gut Mann*, even if she had no interest in him. He'd acted kindly toward Chloe, nothing more.

She smiled more genuinely at him. "How are things at the feedstore?"

"Good. Good. I've always liked working there with my *Bruders*."

"It is fortunate that you all get along so well." Becca loved and liked her own siblings, but she knew that not all families shared this.

"*Yah*. We do get along well." Thad nodded and smiled widely. "I was startled, though, that Saul Stutzman came there to see me the other day."

Looking up quickly from smoothing her skirt, Becca said, "Saul?"

"Yes, he is your brother's good friend, isn't he?"

"Yes," she said, looking down at her lap again.

"I thought so."

Thad shifted in his chair, his movement drawing her gaze. "Becca?"

Seeing that Thad had turned toward her and was now leaning in her direction, she knew something was coming, but had no idea what.

"Becca, I must admit that what he said had me thinking," Thad said, looking at her with an earnest expression.

"It did?" She didn't know what else to say.

"*Yah*." He spoke with strong resolution. "I joined the church just recently and...and it's time for me to start thinking about the future."

The decision in his voice and the ardent way he look at her left Becca feeling uneasy.

"What exactly did Saul say?"

"I have no idea why, but Saul came by just to talk of you."

"Of me?" Hearing her reaction, she wished the question hadn't come out with a squeak.

"*Yah*, it was a little odd, but he stopped by the feedstore and told me that you'd—excuse me for speaking plainly—that you'd be a good wife for a *Mann*." He blushed a little as he ended this speech. "And then he left the store."

"Saul came just for that?" Becca couldn't help that her heart beat faster at this news. It was hard to wrap her head around what Thad was saying. Why would Saul do such a thing?

When Thad left a half hour later, she felt good that she'd convinced him that they two would never be more than friends. She just couldn't now see herself with him and Becca acknowledged that her competition with Chloe had taken precedence in her mind. Thad had never really been a real consideration.

"I told you Saul has feelings for you," Abby commented, pushing open the screen door as the two sisters watched Thad's buggy leaving.

"You were listening to what Thad said," Becca concluded without heat.

"Well, the door—and the windows—were opened and the two of you sat on the porch. It wasn't hard to hear everything."

Becca nodded. "I suppose not."

"I'm glad you offered him some of the lemonade that was there on the table. He could hardly have missed it…and he seems like a nice enough *Mann*."

Sighing, Becca looked pensively at the butterfly spreading its wings as it paused on the pink blossoms of the Joe Pye weed that huddled next to a corner of the porch. "*Yah*, but he's not my *Mann*."

"You need to talk to Saul," her sister observed.

"I've talked to Saul many times," Becca hedged, wondering still if her sister might be right.

"Talk to him again," Abby directed. "As I said, I'm convinced he has feelings for you…and I'm certain that you love him, too."

Becca stared at her sister, unable to deny that she loved Saul. In the past few weeks, Saul had become…different. Not just her brother's friend. Not as brooding and distant.

"How will I know if he loves Chloe, not me?"

Abigail smiled. "Pray about it, *Schweschder*. You'll find the way."

Maybe that was the answer, Becca thought. She'd always been so lucky, established in her *familye's* love. It didn't seem like she should have many troubles, but she couldn't see her way now.

Over and over, she'd been taught to turn to *Gott* to help with troubles and questions, even little ones.

Only this didn't feel little. She loved Saul—sometimes remote, sometimes bossy Saul—and she needed *Gott* to help her know how to move forward with this burning sensation in her chest.

The next evening, Becca scooted some fresh-baked cookies onto a plate, hoping the lovely smell of them wafted over to the bunch of *Englischers* crowded around the B & B fireplace.

The place was throwing parties and events more than it ever had and Becca was glad of the work this provided her. Earlier, her boss had told her they were becoming known for Becca's delicious baking. Stammering that *Gott* enabled her skill, she had then subsided in embarrassment.

Bending now to remove several loaves of sweet bread from the oven, she only heard the B & B front door open.

Straightening with cheeks flushed from the hot oven, she stiffened at the startling sight of Saul standing in the front hall, talking to her boss.

Her cheeks growing hotter, she watched in shock as the two *Menner* exchanged words, her boss' face all respectful and attentive as he talked to the tall, broad-chested *Amisch Mann*. Even the *Englischer* group around the fireplace behind her stopped chattering and she knew they were also staring at the Saul.

"I'd like to speak with Becca Zook," she heard him say in a deep, purposeful voice.

Holding her breath for a moment, Becca watched as Saul walked toward her.

He came to stand across the counter from her in the open kitchen. "Becca, we must speak."

All around them, the *Englischers* silently stared.

Acutely aware of her boss standing behind Saul, his avid interest obvious, her heart pounded in her chest and she felt the gazes of the group around the B & B fireplace on them both.

Gulping, she felt frozen at the counter.

"Becca," her boss said, his gaze flashing between her and Saul, "you have a visitor who wants to speak with you."

Saul stood there, his firm, chiseled chin set, wearing his simple, black suit, broad hat dangling from his hand. Waiting.

Her mind presented her with instantly a detailed memory of the last time he'd been here with her in that kitchen. Of the heated moment when he'd shoved her, all covered in cherry juice, into the pantry and then kissed her senseless.

The front porch. She pounced on the thought. They should go to the front porch.

Becca didn't know what he had to say, but whatever it was didn't need to be said here, in front of this crowd of *Englischers*.

Marching around the counter, she reached out to snag Saul's arm as she moved toward the front door with him following as she dragged him out.

"Come out here," she said in a tense voice as she exited the B & B, his sleeve in her hand. Saul came with her out onto the broad, shadowed B & B front porch. The owner had strung what he'd call fairy lights all around the porch posts and across the edging at the top. Even the bushes had lights in them.

Becca rounded to glare at Saul.

"What are you doing here?!" She hissed, her question no less emphatic with the need she felt not to be overheard by the *Englischers* inside, no doubt ears pressed to the doors and windows.

"I went to your *Haus* tonight and, when I found out that you weren't there, but working here. I followed you. You wouldn't talk to me before, but I'm determined you must listen to what I have to say. This has gone on long enough. So, I came to you here," was his blunt response.

Despite the dim lighting, she saw the tension in his jaw and felt the burn of his intense gaze. Something in that gaze—something warm—left her a little breathless.

"Becca, you must let me explain," Saul said flatly. "I have no interest in Chloe. None. I never made up to her and only took her home that night after the Sing to be nice. She acted like her only other option was to walk home in the dark."

"I'll bet she did," Becca returned, in an acid tone. "She would. Could you not tell that Chloe's pursuing you?"

He shook his head dismissively. "I can't read the silly *Maedel's* mind. How could I know that? And it wouldn't matter, anyway. As I said, I have no interest in Chloe Nissly."

"Well, she has a lot of interest in you!" Becca accused, tartly.

"She may, but this is beyond my control," he pointed out with an unanswerable logic. "Besides, I have done nothing to make you doubt my loyalty."

Tears prickled behind her eyes. "You know I forced you into this pretense. That alone gives you reason to try to get back at me."

She blinked back the moisture in her eyes, glad that the light from a nearby window fell over him, not her.

He made an exasperated sound. "Becca, you should know I don't work that way."

"How am I to know that!" The question started out loud, but she lowered her voice, knowing the inhabitants of the B & B probably had their ears perked.

Standing there on the painted boards of the wide porch, Saul looked at her, pressure in his chest. He'd come there that afternoon to clear the air. At least, that's what he'd told himself.

He wanted her back.

Wanted Becca to be his girl. The idea of the *Maedel* courting with Thad Oberholtzer—or anyone besides himself—was wrong.

Talking about how he felt wasn't ever easy for Saul. It rarely occurred to him to do this and, when it did, his words seemed to get tangled and clogged in his throat. It had to be done now, though. In his prayers, *Gott* left him with the same message on his

144

heart. He had to talk to Becca. Had to tell her how he felt. He'd not be able to tolerate her marrying some other *Mann*.

"I need to tell you," he said jerkily. "I need to talk to you Becca."

She stared at him. "Tell me what? If it's about Chloe, I don't think I want to hear."

"No," Saul impatiently waved aside the subject of the other girl. "This has nothing to do with her."

"Then what?"

"I don't care about everyone knowing what I did to the *Englischer's* tires," he said bluntly. "I never did."

"You didn't?" she asked, looking astonished. "Then-then why did you agree to my plan?"

Saul looked down briefly, before lifting to determinedly meeting her gaze. "Because I didn't want you asking another *Mann* to fulfill your silly plan."

Confusion played over her features. "I don't understand. Why not?"

Knowing he couldn't just reach out and kiss her, using action to show his meaning, Saul decided to break the truth down as simply as he could.

"Because, Becca, you've become more to me than just Adam's silly pest of a sister. You are a pest sometimes, but you're important to me for just yourself." There. He'd said it. The words that had been circling in his head for days.

She squeaked, "I am?"

"*Yah*." He looked into her blue, blue eyes. "You are. You've thought so little of yourself for so long that you can't see the truth. You're not perfect, but none of us are. You're not less than Abby. You don't need to compete with Chloe. You're wonderful just as you are."

"Saul," she said hope mingling with disbelief in her face, "are you telling me that you have…feelings for me?"

Reaching out for her, Saul pulled Becca up close. Growling, he said, "It's gone beyond that for me. I liked you—more than liked you—when I agreed to this all."

"Oh, Saul," she breathed, her face tipped up to his.

He bent then and kissed her.

"Oh!" Becca exclaimed when he pulled back, the listening *Englischers* inside the B & B, totally forgotten.

She didn't resist when he kissed her again, responding fervently to his embrace.

"I love you, Becca," Saul said in a ragged voice when their lips finally separated. "I've loved you all along, I think."

"Oh!" she exclaimed, bursting then into tears.

Saul pushed back, staring at her with one eyebrow comically cocked.

Becca sniffled, throwing herself back against his chest and saying in muffled words that she loved him, too. So much.

"Then, stop crying," he directed, "and let me kiss you again."

"You always annoyed and upset me more than anyone else," she hiccupped with her tears, "and you made me laugh. I've always cared about you. More than I ever wanted you to know. No wonder I asked you to pretend court with me. I think I've loved you all my life!"

She beamed up at him in the dim light.

Saul kissed her again, this time more thoroughly. When he then held her against his thundering heart, he said. "I have loved you, all this time. I realize that now."

Still locked in his arms, *Kapp* now askew, she asked, "Even when we were *Youngies*? Is that why you teased me so mercilessly? Mocking me when I got caught in the blackberry bush and laughing when I fell in the river?"

"I was kind of a jerk" he admitted, and then chuckled, "although those both were just funny situations and I stole your bread in the kitchen because it's good."

Somehow, they'd moved to occupy the wide swing on the B & B porch, Saul keeping his arms around Becca.

"My bread's really good," she responded smugly.

"And you're so modest and godly about it," he observed dryly.

She snuggled into his arms. "And the most wonderful thing about this is that I'm so happy with you that I don't even care about Chloe. I just don't care."

Becca reached up to kiss him again.

Thanks so much for purchasing Becca's Boy! If you enjoyed this book, please consider leaving a review for Becca's Boy, Book 1, Amish Sisters Marry Romance Series! Authors live and die by reviews and I would be very grateful if you would do me the honor of leaving one. Thanks in advance. I so appreciate it!

.

Carol Rose

Glossary of Amish Terms:

Amisch—how the Amish refer to themselves
Bickle- pickle
Bisskatz—skunk
Bopplin--babies
Bruder—brother
Buwe--boy
Daed—dad
Eldre—parents
Englischer—anyone who isn't Amish
Familye—family
Frau—wife
Geschwischder—Brothers and sisters
Goedenavond—good evening
Goedemorgen—good morning
Gott—God
Grossmammi—grandmother
Gut—good
Haus—house
Kinder/Kinner—children
Liebling—sweetheart, darling, honey
Maedel—young woman
Mamm-mother
Mann—man
Menner—men
Neh--no
Schweschder—sister
Schmaert—smart
Schlang--snake
Yah—yes

About the Author

Rose Doss is an award-winning romance author. She has written thirty-one romance novels. Her books have won numerous awards, including a final in the prestigious Romance Writers of America Golden Heart Award.

A frequent speaker at writers' groups and conferences, she has taught workshops on characterization and, creating and resolving conflict. She works full time as a therapist.

Her husband and she married when she was only nineteen and he was barely twenty-one, proving that early marriage can make it, but only if you're really lucky and very persistent. They went through college and grad school together. She not only loves him still, all these years later, and she still likes him—which she says is sometimes harder. They have two funny, intelligent and highly accomplished daughters and three granddaughters, whose names all start with E like their great-grandmother, Eloise.

Rose loves writing and hopes you enjoy reading her work.

Amish Romances:

Amish By Choice (Amish Vows Romance, Prequel)
Amish Renegade(Amish Vows Romance, Bk 1)
Amish Princess(Amish Vows Romance, Bk 2)
Amish Heartbreaker(Amish Vows Romance, Bk 3)
Amish Spinster(Amish Vows Romance, Bk 4)
Amish Prodigal (Amish Vows Romance, Bk 5)
Amish Rogue(Amish Vows Romance, BK 6)

www.rosedoss.com
www.twitter.com - carolrose@carolrosebooks
https://www.facebook.com/carol.rose.author

Made in the USA
Middletown, DE
17 January 2025

69679700R00086